I0666269

THEIR WORLD

HER ROYAL HAREM: LILY
BOOK TWO

CATHERINE BANKS

TURBO KITTEN INDUSTRIES

Their World by Catherine Banks

Copyright © 2025 Catherine Banks

All rights reserved.

Cover design by Covers by Juan

Character art and break art by Cyan Covers and Designs

Chapter background art by Artscandare

Formatted by Turbo Kitten Industries™

Published by Turbo Kitten Industries™

Turbo Kitten Industries™

P.O. Box 5041, Galt, CA 95632

To Avery for his support and love.

CHAPTER
ONE

Being teleported to another world was the start to several adventure movies I had watched growing up. I never thought it would happen to me, though.

I stood atop a ridge overlooking what must have been grasslands before it had been set on fire. There were a few trees that dotted the ridge and the field below, but they were blackened husks.

The demon world looked like it was dying, or had been burned significantly and left to die. I didn't see any water source, which worried me. I needed water to survive. Did the demons not drink water?

This was definitely near the spot the hellhound pup had come through that we'd had the video of. When he'd run through, several hellhounds and a humanoid had been there, so it was probably a good idea to get away from this area. I wasn't sure how the portals worked, so I didn't know if one would open here again or not.

The spell that had paralyzed me had stopped working as soon as I came here, so I was able to stand and move again.

Taking off at an easy jog, I headed towards the large spire that I had a suspicion was a castle.

There wasn't cover in this area, so I moved as quickly as I could across the burnt and desolate lands towards what looked like an area that used to be a forest and would provide me at least a little cover.

"I hope everyone back home is safe," I whispered to myself.

A screech from my right alerted me just before a bat-demon flew towards me and tried to grab me with its sharp talons.

Ducking down and rolling to the left, I avoided its talons and resumed running.

"Back off or I'll eat you," I threatened. "I don't know when I'll get a meal and you'd fill my belly for at least a few days." It was a hollow threat. If I ate it, I'd have to lie still while I digested it for at least a day, which would leave me very vulnerable.

The forest of burnt trees loomed in front of me, and I ran straight in without inspection. The trees provided enough coverage to help me hide even as burned as they were due to their height. The only problem was my footsteps were extraordinarily loud due to the crispy burnt pieces of bark on the ground.

A familiar yip caught my attention and I slowed as the hellhound pup ran to me, barking and jumping around in a circle happily.

"Hello, boy," I greeted. "How did you find me so quickly?"

He trotted around me and started in the direction I had been headed, looked over his shoulder at me, and barked while wagging his tail.

"You want me to follow?" I asked.

He bobbed his head and jogged away.

I resumed my jog, this time following the hellhound pup, and cringed at how loud I was compared to the pup.

"I might as well be an elephant," I grumbled.

"An elephant would be much more quiet," a deep, male voice said from in front of me. A male humanoid demon stepped in front of me, forcing me to slide to a stop.

"I didn't come here willingly," I said, tensed and ready to fight. "Just let me find a portal and I'll go back home."

The pup sat down between us, his tongue lulling out his mouth as he looked at both of us, completely unbothered by this demon.

The humanoid demon canted his head, his horns sparkling in the low light that filtered through the trees. "The necklace brought you here for a reason. I don't know what that reason is yet, but I'm not gifted with premonitions so it is not for me to know." He shrugged, and I realized I recognized his armor. He was the one that had had a spiked club. He was the one I'd thought was going to kill me right before the necklace teleported me here.

"My family and friends ... are they alive?" I asked, my throat tightening as I prepared for possible bad news.

He straightened. "You may not know much about

demons, but let me tell you this, demon warriors, such as myself, have honor. I did not kill any of your people."

Exhaling in relief, I gave him the distraction he needed to run forward and wrap a strange silver chain around me. As soon as it was around me, I couldn't move or shift or do anything.

Instead of letting me fall to the ground, he caught me and picked me up in a bridal carry. "Now, let's go to my home, so we don't have to continue traipsing through this dead forest. Come, pup."

The pup yipped and followed obediently.

"You have to eat," the demon who had grabbed me two days ago said sternly.

"I don't have to do shit," I snapped back and hissed at him for good measure.

The hellhound pup I had rescued and who I felt had slightly betrayed me, lay on the floor, whining at me with his ears flattened against his head.

"Even Dhun is worried about you," the demon said.

After tying me up in a weird rope, he'd carried me to the spire, which had indeed been a castle made of a strange rock that seemed to absorb all the light around it. All of the demons, no matter their size or shape, bowed to the warrior demon and averted their eyes from looking at me. One demon had peeked at me and the warrior demon had released a vicious growl that had sent them all scurrying away.

The warrior demon put me in a room that rivaled the best hotels I had ever stayed at with a fluffy mattress, huge claw-footed tub in the connected bathroom that had indoor plumbing, and a chaise lounge chair that was perfect for relaxing on.

I continued to stay curled up on the chaise lounge, ignoring them both. As far as I was concerned, the pup was a traitor who had failed to protect me from getting kidnapped by this demon.

"Would you prefer live food? You are a snake shifter from what we saw, so I could find you live food to consume."

There was absolutely zero judgment in his words, just genuine concern.

Was I going about this all wrong? Should I be trying to make him my friend or ally? He hadn't done anything aggressive since bringing me here. If he really wasn't my enemy, then I needed to alter my plan.

Sitting up, I asked, "When can I go home?"

He shrugged. "That's not up to me."

"Who is it up to? Let me talk to them."

"It's up to fate," he answered. "The necklace will send you back home when it's time, or a portal will open in front of you."

Dropping my head into my hands, I sighed dramatically. "If I eat food here, will I be stuck here?"

"What? Why would you be stuck here?"

"There are stories of people eating food after going through a portal and then being unable to return to their home. I just want to make sure that's not going to happen here," I explained.

"That's absurd," he whispered. "What kind of worlds have you been to?"

Looking up, I saw his horrified face and burst into laughter.

He stood on the plush grey carpet before the chaise lounge, watching me curiously.

"What's your name?" I asked once I'd stopped laughing.

"I am King Jolmach of the Demons, First of my Name, Fourth to Reign." He bowed with a flourish.

My eyes widened as I realized that, of course, the man who lived in this tower and had the demons bowing would be their king.

"It's an honor to meet you, King Jolmach," I replied.

"May I know your name?" he asked.

"Oh. I thought you knew already," I admitted and stood. Why did they know about me, but not know my name? "I am Princess Liliana Rubyserpent of the Hybrids, adopted daughter of the King and Queen of the Hybrids." I curtsied, but kept my head raised as I had been taught never to bow my head to anyone except *my* king and queen.

He reached out slowly, took one of my hands, raised it, and kissed my knuckles. "It is an honor to meet you, Princess Liliana Rubyserpent."

My heart beat a bit faster, and I took a moment to study his face, noting that while it wasn't traditionally handsome, he wasn't bad looking either. Once again, I got the feeling that he was like me, a hybrid shifter, or something because there was a weird connection between us. The same strange connection I felt to Dhun.

"Will you eat?" he asked. Glancing at Dhun he said, "He won't eat until you do, so you're really punishing both of you."

I had a feeling he was playing at my emotions, but I nodded, then pointed at him and said, "But if I end up stuck here, I'm going to make your life miserable."

He smiled and said, "Noted." Walking over to the door, he pulled it open and bowed as he waved me through. "After you, Princess."

Dhun hopped up, ears perked and tail wagging, and trotted behind me as I walked out of the room and into the hallway lined with torches along the wall in grooves that had been cut into the strange stone. Some of them had mana stones at the bases as well.

King Jolmach walked beside me, arms lose at his side, but his body was rigid.

"So, where is your queen?" I asked. "Or prince or advisors?"

The castle was eerily empty as we walked down the hallway and entered a kitchen, also empty of others.

"I have no queen and no spawn. I have military advisors, but they are in a room together discussing strategies to present to me, so you can meet them later." He went to a rectangular stone box and opened it, shocking me as cool air like a refrigerator came out.

It seemed we were completely wrong about the demons. If I was stuck here for who knew how long, it would be the perfect opportunity to learn more about them. To have an accurate record to somehow send back home.

"So, you cook for yourself?" I asked. "You don't have a chef to do that for you?"

He pulled out a box of my favorite brand of chicken nuggets and a bottle of ketchup that was definitely from my world. At my shocked expression, he asked, "Did you see the desolation of the lands before the forest and what remains of the forest?"

I nodded.

"That's how ninety percent of our world is now."

"Is that why you're invading our world? Because you don't have resources for your people?"

He frowned, put the chicken nuggets back, and said, "Let me show you something."

Heading out a side door I hadn't noticed, the stone all looked alike, so it was hard to see the seams. He led me to a balcony that overlooked a city made of small houses and a few two to three story buildings. Demons in all shapes and sizes, including children with their parents, walked or flew around the city.

"This is our main city, Obselk. One of three cities that remain now. We used to have dozens of cities. Millions of demons. We've tried everything, but our world continues to die. We continue to try to take things from your world and plant them here, but it's to no avail."

"Take things from our world?" I asked, frowning. As far as I knew, no one had ever mentioned demons taking things back through the portals.

"If you aren't looking for something, it is easy to miss,

Princess. When a portal opens and we go through, we aren't doing so aimlessly. We take food, useful items, and plants."

My eyes widened. They had been stealing things to sustain their people?

"So far, every plant we bring back dies after it's planted and even if we bring a potted plant here, it will die within a few days, leaves burned. Our environment is no longer habitable for plant life."

"The portals opening in the city, you go into the stores and take items," I realized.

He nodded, and we walked back to the kitchen. He held up the chicken nugget box. "Like these."

"Why not try to speak to our kings to work something out? Why attack our people?"

Scoffing, he shook his head. "Your people kill mine before a chance is even given. It wasn't until we were able to see you that we realized there might be another way. Even then, your people killed dozens of mine."

All of this seemed like a huge misunderstanding that could be worked out with communication and aid. One thing he'd said bothered me, though.

"See me? How did you see me?"

"Our Grand Advisor was able to use his powers to find you, to show us images of you, and advise me that you were the one we needed to learn about the other world."

They wanted to use me to learn about our world? Why me?

"You will meet the Grand Advisor soon, but he is not available currently."

"How do the portals work?" I asked. "Do you choose where they open? Is it you that opens them?"

Jolmach sighed and shook his head. "No, I have no control over the portals. My people are spread around, watching for the portals, for their chance to jump through them and grab supplies from your world."

Jolmach shook out some nuggets onto a metal cooking sheet, exhaled fire onto the nuggets, grabbed a plate, and put the now cooked nuggets onto it. "I know it's not the most luxurious meal—"

"It's great, thank you," I said and popped a nugget into my mouth.

He watched me as I ate, brows furrowed. "You're no longer angry?"

Wiping my mouth with the back of my hand, I explained, "I thought you were holding me prisoner. So I assumed you were my enemy." Canting my head, I said, "However, it seems that we could be allies, and I might be able to help you."

"You would help us take over your world?" he asked and arched a brow.

My brows furrowed. "Take over the world?"

"How else will my people survive?"

"What if we can help you without that being necessary?" I asked.

He shook his head. "This world is dying. We must leave."

"Have you seen any other worlds through the portal?"

"No, only yours."

"There has to be another way, other than you taking over my world."

"The council and Grand Advisor are certain that we must take it. They said if there were another way, they would have thought of it already or been shown it by the gods. None has been presented."

"And yet, a princess of that world is here, something your council didn't know would happen previously. There is almost always another way." No matter what, I had to convince him not to continue with this path. I had to protect my family, my friends, and my world.

I would protect them no matter what it took.

"Come, you must be tired," Jolmach said, clearly wanting to end the conversation. "I'll take you back to your room." At the room, he paused by the door and said, "While I am not keeping you prisoner here, I am keeping you here for your protection. Not all of the beings are as intelligent as me or Dhun. Those who did not see me with you will not know to leave you unharmed. If you wander alone, you will be in danger, so please, let me know if you wish to go somewhere, okay?"

Smiling, I nodded and said, "Understood."

He frowned, clearly not believing me. "Is there anything you need before I retire?"

"A notebook or paper and a writing utensil?" I asked. "Oh, and water."

Opening the door, he whistled and Dhun ran out. He squatted, said something to Dhun, and stood. "Dhun will fetch the items you need. Please stay in the room while he is gone."

"Thank you. Have a good night, King Jolmach."

He bowed and said, "Have a good evening, Princess."

Sitting back on the chaise lounge, I went over my four new goals.

One, learn as much about this world and its people as I could. The more information I had, the more prepared I would be.

Two, get in touch with my family and let them know I was safe for now. Knowing my family and friends, they were freaking out and trying to rescue me.

Three, find a way to prevent the demons from trying to take over my world.

And the most important goal.

Four, stay alive.

CHAPTER
TWO

Dhun had returned about an hour later carrying items in a bag that was secured to stay on his back. I assumed King Jolmach had attached it, but didn't bother asking.

While he'd been gone, I had taken my phone out and tried to call or send a message, but there was no service. Did it only work when a portal was open and near you? I'd been able to watch Dhun through the video call for about thirty seconds before the phone had been destroyed.

I drafted an email to go to my entire family and the trio, so if a portal did open and I wasn't able to make it through, maybe the email would send during that window of time.

The book I'd been provided was leather bound, had blank, lined pages, and had a price sticker from one of our popular bookstore chains on the back.

"Using stolen goods," I whispered, and shook my head. "I never thought I'd see the day. Mom would be so disappointed."

Dhun canted his head, looking confused.

The first lefthand page I titled "Hierarchy", the second left hand page I titled "King Jolmach". I gave each item the two pages, so I had enough room for notes. About the middle of the book, I titled it "Creatures" and gave each creature a page to draw them as best as I could, note their attributes, and if I was stuck here long enough, whatever else I learned about them.

With Dhun in the room, I was able to draw a hellhound a bit better than the ones I'd seen for a short time, since I could stare at him as I drew. He seemed to realize I wanted him to stay still, so he sat straight and still, only moving his eyes to look at the page. Once finished, I showed it to him.

He yipped and danced around in a circle.

"I take it you think I did a good job drawing you?"

He bobbed his head.

"Tomorrow, I think we should walk around the castle a bit," I said. "So, I can see the other types of demons." And so I could map out the castle and draw the floorplan.

Dhun panted and curled up on the rug.

"Okay, fine, bed time it is," I said and closed the book. Laying on the bed, I wondered what everyone back home was doing.

Would my parents be able to sleep? Would my brother and Maya console each other? Would the trio be causing havoc somewhere?

Knowing the trio, Mason was trying to jump through the nearest portal while Kayden was holding him back until they developed a plan.

Imagining that scenario put a smile on my face and allowed me to fall asleep.

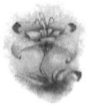

THE NEXT MORNING, King Jolmach knocked on my door and escorted me back to the kitchen for breakfast. He pushed a plate of meat and scrambled eggs towards me.

"Did you sleep well?" he asked.

I nodded. "I did, how about you?"

Simple conversation would help keep things civil between us and hopefully keep his guard down to give me as much information as possible.

"About as normal," he said with a shrug.

"Is there a plan for today?" I asked. "Would it be okay to take Dhun with me and explore the castle? I swear not to leave it."

He stared at me a moment, looked down at Dhun, and said, "I have to speak with my council, so I won't be able to escort you. If you stay in the castle, you should be safe. I'll send one of the warriors with you just in case. Dhun is still young and inexperienced."

Dhun huffed and lowered his head, his ears drooping sadly.

"Do the other warriors talk, too?" I asked.

"If they choose to," he said with a half-smile.

"King Jolmach, have you—"

"Just Jol, please," he said, interrupting me.

I smiled. "Jol, have you heard from your Grand Advisor?"

He shook his head. "Not yet. I'm sure he'll reach out

soon." Looking down at Dhun, he said, "Ensure you show her the boundaries of the castle and don't stray from them. Tensions are high amongst our people right now."

Dhun barked his acknowledgment.

"Do you have communication devices?" I asked. "Like phones or other electronics?"

"We have magic stones that we can use to hear each other across far distances," he answered. "Are you wanting one?"

"I thought it might put you more at ease if I had one, in case I needed to call for your help," I said and shrugged. "It was just a thought."

"I was going to suggest it, actually. I'm glad we seem to be on the same page. I have to admit, I was worried when I first met you and how you acted the first couple of days, but it's refreshing to have someone who can adapt so quickly to the situation. Perhaps the Grand Advisor really did know you were the person we needed." He pulled out a clear teal stone and held it out on his palm. "You just grip it, picture the person you want to speak to, and it will send your voice to them."

"To the stone you have?"

He tapped his temple. "To their mind."

Was this how the person who said I was going to become a goddess had communicated with me?

"So, it wasn't you who communicated with me previously?" I asked.

He scowled. "Someone communicated with you?"

I waved my hand and smiled. "Forget about it. Where's the warrior who will go with us?"

Pulling a stone from his pocket, he closed his eyes and said, "Come to the kitchen."

Several minutes later, a warrior demon, a bit shorter than Jol, walked in and bowed to him.

"This is Zoman. Zoman, this is Princess Liliana. I want you to shadow her in case anyone tries to harm her. She and Dhun have agreed to stay in the castle and only explore the interior of the castle, so they shouldn't need your help, but it will make us both feel better to have you there as well."

Zoman dipped his head and bowed. "As you wish, my king." His voice was softer than I expected, somewhat melodic, and it was obvious he had great respect for Jol. Once again, I felt a sense of familiarity, of pack, like he was a hybrid shifter.

"I need to grab a couple things from my room first," I said and looked down at Dhun. "Can you carry things in your bag for me?" He still had the bag across his back that he'd used to bring the book and other items to me.

Dhun barked his agreement.

"Great!" I said and turned to Zoman. "I will do my best to avoid causing you trouble today."

He just stared at me without responding.

Got it, I wasn't his king and he clearly didn't like me.

Jol said, "I'll come find you for lunch."

"Okay," I said with a smile and headed out of the kitchen and in the direction I thought went to my room.

Dhun trotted at my side, more pep in his step than I'd seen so far.

"You seem to be in a good mood," I commented.

He yipped his agreement.

"He thinks it is a great honor to be assigned to you," Zoman said. "He thinks being your friend will boost his status amongst the hounds here more than it has already."

"Is that why they left you alone the last time I saw you? Because you'd stayed with me for a bit?"

He barked an acknowledgment.

"Well, I'm glad I could help you," I said and smiled down at him. Stopping at a turn, I looked both ways. "I think I'm lost," I admitted.

Dhun trotted to the left and looked back to make sure I followed.

"Thanks," I said and followed him.

I put the book, pen, and water bottle into Dhun's pack and put my phone in my pocket.

"Ready? I asked Dhun.

He barked his agreement and trotted to the door, where Zoman waited for us.

"Sorry you got babysitting duty," I said as Dhun led the way down the hallway to start my castle tour.

"The king gave me an order and I will follow it, no matter how menial it may seem to others," he replied.

"You respect your king," I stated with a nod. "That must mean he is a good king."

"Without his leadership, we would have all died without resources to survive."

The resources they were stealing from my world.

"When did all this devastation happen?" I asked. "Was there a battle or something that destroyed the area?"

"It started with a battle, then the gods cursed us, and we

all would have died if the Grand Advisor and King hadn't come up with this new plan."

If the portals were random, how did they plan to get to my world to fight? Would they just continue sending as many through at one time as they could? Or had Jol lied about not controlling the portals? That large one they'd come through with the giant werewolf-demon had seemed unique and it had stayed open long enough for Jol to go through to fight.

There was definitely more I needed to learn.

Stopping Dhun, I pulled out the book and started drawing the floorplan as we reached the end of this hallway and turned down another. It was odd that we'd walked down a very long hallway that had zero doors, aside from the one bedroom I was using. Unless it was like the door Jol had opened earlier and I just wasn't able to see the seams?

That seemed much more probable.

We got to the end of that hallway, but there were two large glass doors that led to a balcony. I pushed open the doors and stepped out, closing my eyes and tilting my face up to enjoy the sunlight. I took a deep breath and immediately regretted it as a foul odor filled my nose.

Opening my eyes, I walked to the edge of the balcony and looked out across the field we faced. Demons milled about, going about their day, but many looked almost robotic as they walked.

"Your water supply didn't suffer?" I asked.

"Thankfully, it has only had a slight decrease in amount, but the freshness is still good. We do have to travel deeper to obtain the clean water, but we have developed rope and pulley systems to bring it to the surface," Zoman answered.

So it was just living plants that wouldn't survive. I wasn't a super talented elf, but when I had a chance, I would try to use my magic to heal the land, to see if it was possible. If I was stuck here anyway, where was the harm?

One of the demons walking down below wasn't a type I had seen before. I flipped through the book to a page for drawing the creatures and drew as much as I could tell from this distance.

I sensed Zoman get closer and a second later he said, "You're drawing us?"

"Each type," I said with a nod.

"Why?"

"I'm trying to understand you all, and the more I know about you, the better I'll understand." I flipped back to the picture of Dhun I'd drawn and showed it to him. "What do you call him?"

"Dhun," he replied.

I shook my head. "Not him specifically, but his type."

"Oh, we don't have names for the differences in appearance. We're all just demons." He shrugged.

Interesting.

"You have different names for your people?" he asked.

I nodded. "Dragons, werewolves, mages, elves, humans, and hybrids."

"Which are you?" he asked.

"Hybrid," I answered with a smile. "Because I'm a mixture of multiple races." Realization hit me. "How did you learn our language?"

"The Grand Advisor found items to teach us and now it's

required for those with higher intelligence to learn, so we are able to communicate with those in your world," he explained. He seemed like he wanted to say more, but turned away instead.

We continued on, going down a stairwell to the floor below the one we had just explored.

"Can we actually start from the first floor?" I asked.

Dhun barked his confirmation and continued down the stairwell until he reached the first floor, then went down a few hallways so we stood at the front door of the castle. He looked at me and I nodded. "Perfect, thank you, Dhun."

Turned out there was a room with a throne and seats for Jol to hold audience with his people.

"We haven't really used this room much since the war," Zoman admitted.

Hard to hold court with your people when you were trying to simply survive.

As I stared at the throne, an odd sense of familiarity filled me. There were no designs on it, but there were a few mana stones embedded into it. What did it mean?

There were a few rooms that Dhun pushed his head on the door to open and show me, like a large meeting room with a huge table that had at least fourteen chairs around it. Following him up a particularly narrow staircase that seemed to go up at least four floors, we stepped out onto the roof of the castle.

"Whoa," I whispered as I grabbed my hair to keep it from whipping me in the face. From up here, I could see miles around the castle.

Most of it was burned or dead, a blackened landscape

that showed why they were becoming more desperate to find a solution to save themselves.

Far in the distance, I saw several giant demon creatures, like the one that had come through the portal after me that Dad had fought. There were a couple werewolf looking ones, a giant version of the bull-headed demons, and one that looked like a T-rex, but with bright blue fur.

"Do those giant ones ever attack the cities?" I asked curiously.

Zoman shook his head. "No, they are herd creatures and prefer to stay far away. Once, they tried to attack the city, but King Jolmach defeated their leader and the rest fled, never returning."

"What do they eat? There doesn't seem to be a food source for them."

"Other demons," Zoman answered. "Those who are unfortunate enough to venture into their territory. There are many demons without humanity, with very little intelligence, and they live out there, in what we call the wildlands."

Being forced to survive by eating your own people? How terrible!

What could I do to help? How could I help them and protect my world simultaneously?

There had to be a way. I had to think of a way. What good was I as a princess if I couldn't figure this out?

Far in the distance, I thought I saw a glint of green, an aura of life, but when I blinked, it was gone. Had I imagined it?

"Can you take me to a spot that used to be a garden or where plants used to grow?" I asked Dhun.

"There are none within the castle," Zoman said quickly.

"Is it possible for you to take me there?" I requested. "If you need to check with Jol—"

"King Jolmach," Zoman snapped.

"Please? I want to see if I can help," I explained.

"Help?" Zoman asked and both he and Dhun canted their heads, brows furrowed. "How could you help?"

"I'm not certain I can, but I'd like to try. It's not like I could make things worse, right?" I gave him my best smile, but he still looked extremely skeptical.

Zoman pulled out a communication stone from his pocket and turned away, whispering to it. After several minutes, he turned back and said, "It will have to wait. The Grand Advisor is ready to see you now."

THREE

Zoman led the way back down through the castle to the large meeting room. When we stepped inside, instead of being empty like it had been when we visited, it was full of humanoid demons All had horns, dark eyes, and a few had tails that moved back and forth in agitation.

Every single one in the room felt like a hybrid to me. Was it just a similarity? Or were they originally from our world?

Many gave me curious stares, while a few were openly glaring.

Jol stood beside an older looking demon with horns that curved up from the sides of his head. He wore a hooded top with the hood up and the horns coming out through holes in the hood. His grey beard was a few inches long and his eyes were slightly red. He sat in the chair on Jol's right and tapped his finger impatiently.

"I apologize for the delay, Your Majesty, but we were on the roof when you notified me," Zoman explained with a bow.

Jol stood and said, "Princess Liliana, please meet our Grand Advisor."

So, he didn't have a name? Just 'Grand Advisor'? He was like our elders, it seemed.

The Grand Advisor held out his hand, palm down. I stared at it for a second, unsure what I was supposed to do. So, I shook it like I would anyone else's hand.

"It's a pleasure to meet you," I said with a warm smile. Through our joined hands, I felt a tingling sensation, a feeling that he was a hybrid like me, and something else ... something dark, like a feeling of bloodlust.

He frowned at our joined hands, but raised his eyes and smiled. "We've been waiting a long time for you, Princess."

"Yes, about that. I'd love to hear how it was decided that I was the one you wanted to speak to instead of one of the kings or queens and discuss possible solutions to all of this."

"Sit," Jol said and indicated the empty chair on his left, across from the Grand Advisor.

"We were debriefed on the fight that happened right before you were teleported," Grand Advisor said. "Were those all of your strongest fighters? Or are there more who were not present?"

Really? He thought I was just going to give up all our secrets? Did he think I was a moron? I wasn't a child, for goodness' sake.

"We have a lot more," I answered nonchalantly. "We didn't call them as we didn't deem it necessary."

He scowled deeply, as did Jol.

"You could have been killed," Jol said softly. "Had I

wanted to, I could have crushed your head and they would not have been able to stop it."

I rolled my eyes. "That's what you *think*, but you have no idea what they're capable of, especially if it's to protect their family."

"What are they capable of?" Grand Advisor asked.

"Why haven't you tried to open communication with us if you learned our language?" I asked instead of answering.

"It seems each time we tried, the people were not the ones we actually needed to communicate with," Jol said. "They fled in terror or attacked as soon as we stepped out of the portal."

"Did you go, or did one of the others in this room?" I asked and looked around the room.

They all shook their heads.

"You might have had better luck sending someone who looked more like us. I know that sounds incredibly racist, but the hellhounds and bull-men are frightening to the majority of my people. If you had stepped out of the portal, hands raised, and asked to speak to a king, they would have listened."

"You don't know that for certain," one of them said.

"One of the hunters is incredibly vicious and likes to decapitate our people," one of the others said.

Ah, he was definitely talking about Mason.

"Even he would have stopped if you'd come out with hands raised and spoken. All this time, we thought you couldn't speak our language. We thought your people couldn't communicate or didn't want to, and your only goal was killing us."

"You may think highly of your people, but we have lost hundreds of our own by sending them," Grand Advisor said.

"Was it you I spoke to before I was teleported?" I asked him instead of reacting to the taunt.

His eyes widened a moment and then he nodded and his lip twitched, but he refrained from smiling.

"What is a goddess to you? What did you mean by that?" Now that I knew our language was not their first, I hoped to get an explanation to help me better understand what he meant.

"Goddess?" Jol asked, looking between us. "What are you talking about?"

"That is something we can discuss in private," Grand Advisor said and smiled softly.

Red flags sprang up in my mind. This man was dangerous and definitely up to something. He was keeping things from Jol, which was the largest red flag of all.

"I wouldn't think you would keep something so important from your king," I said with a sweet smile. If I could sow seeds of uncertainty amongst them, perhaps I could delay the battle and have more time to find a solution. I wasn't the best when it came to politics, but I had tried to pay attention to all the discussions and arguments that were had.

Grand Advisor waved his hand dismissively. "It's not something our king needs to worry over. He is busy enough preparing for the upcoming war."

"You speak of the war as though it is definite, but what if there is another way?"

"I have seen it," Grand Advisor said and looked at his fingernails as though bored. "It will happen."

"Ah, so you have premonitions as well," I said with a nod of understanding.

His head jerked up. "'As well?'"

"It is one of my powers," I said and copied him, looked at my fingernails and rubbed them on my shirt before raising my head again.

He looked furious.

"You have the power of sight?" Jol asked, eyes wide.

Looking around, I realized every demon there was shocked.

"Among others," I said nonchalantly, with a shrug.

"And you are not an advisor to your people?" Jol asked.

"I advise them if I need to," I explained.

"And you have not seen our war?" Grand Advisor asked, a brow arched. "Perhaps that means your premonition powers are not as strong."

"It could also mean that it is not a certainty. The decisions of many will affect the future."

He sighed and shook his head. "You are very young. It seems you do not have the sight as I have it."

Shrugging, I said, "I don't know what your powers are like to compare them to mine. Just as you don't know what my powers are like. Though, I find it curious that you advised me to accept the shadow powers so willingly. Did you know what they were? Did it come from this necklace?" I reached up, pulled the necklace from beneath my shirt, and stroked a finger down the gem.

Grand Advisor scowled and looked, uncertain. Had it not been him who communicated with me after all?

"Shadow powers?" Jol asked, looking back and forth between the Grand Advisor and me.

Holding my arm out, I summoned the power and the shadow snake with ruby eyes swirled out from my chest and coiled around my arm, resting its head in the palm of my hand.

Jol stood from his seat, nearly knocking the chair over in his haste. "What is this?" he growled. "Did you know she has this power?"

Grand Advisor looked just as surprised as Jol.

"Once upon a time, there lived a little girl," I began and stood, walking around the room with the shadow snake slithering from one arm, up around my neck, to the other arm, and back. "Her mother was gone when she was just a baby, so her father was her only parent. Her father got into a fight and died. A beautiful woman and her mate, King and Queen of the Hybrids, took the little girl and adopted her, making her a princess. While visiting an island thought to be vacant, they encountered friends and enemies. The enemies tried to use a spell that would have had catastrophic results, possibly taking the adoptive mother away from her. So, the little girl jumped into the way, getting hit by the spell instead. The spell was a personality altering spell. It caused the little girl to be angry and a darkness blossomed within her." Thinking angry thoughts, I made my hair glow, and all of their eyes widened. I skipped the part about sharing the darkness with the guys, since that was a bit too personal and painful for me still. "Friends gifted the princess with a pretty necklace." I touched the necklace on my chest. "The necklace seemed to draw demon portals to her and draw the attention of demons as well." The Grand Advisor shifted in his seat nervously as Jol looked at him. "Then, the darkness within her, the power became too great and one day after her twenty-fifth birthday, the power exploded out of her." I mimed exploding with my hands. "A voice told her to accept it and become a goddess. She accepted it and the power now lives in this form." I held up the snake, and it rose taller, hissing at everyone. "And that is how the beautiful princess got these powers. The end." Looking at the Grand Advisor, I arched a brow and asked, "Or is it? Would you care to fill in the blanks? Why does King Jolmach think this necklace has something to do with fate?"

"The one fated to come here received that necklace," Grand Advisor answered and smoothed his shirt down.

I wasn't certain I was correct, but I continued with my thought process, trusting my instincts. "Fated? You gave it to a demon, knowing my childhood friends are the ones who fight the demons, and your premonition showed you that they would give it to me. What else did your premonition show you?"

"Your friends gave it to you?" Jol asked.

I nodded. "As a courting gift," I said to really throw a wrench in the Grand Advisor's claims.

Jol scowled. "A *courting* gift?"

Grand Advisor's eyes narrowed.

"We had made a pact to become mates at twenty-five, but my parents required us to court first, so they gave me the necklace as a gift. To show me that they thought of me even when out battling demons."

"So, you weren't the one who found it then, which means

you aren't the one meant to be here," one of the other demons said and looked at the Grand Advisor.

"No, she is the one meant to be here," he said with certainty. "She is the one we need here."

"And I am here," I said. "Tell me what your premonition of the war looked like."

"It was of us winning," he said vaguely. "And I had another premonition shortly after of us walking through your world while your people cowered in fear."

"Did your premonition of you winning have King Jolmach standing over me in his armor with his spiked mace in his hand while my family watched?"

His eyes widened. "Perhaps."

I turned to Jol and said, "Isn't that exactly what happened before the necklace teleported me here?"

Jol nodded with a deep frown. "It is."

Turning back to the Grand Advisor I asked, "Is this necklace really a communication device and one you can use to teleport me?"

He stood with a snarl. "This is outrageous. You dare to question me, the Grand Advisor? I am the reason we've survived as long as we have. I am the reason we're able to utilize the portals."

My hair had started glowing and I tried to stop it, but the more his lies fell into line with my thought process, the brighter it glowed. "Utilize the portals you create, you mean?" I asked. "My adoptive mom can create portals, up to five at a time."

"Explain," Jol demanded and snarled at the Grand Advisor.

"Are you really going to listen to the words of an outsider? A child who knows nothing of our world? I've been doing everything I can to help us. I was put here by the gods."

His body shimmered a moment before starting to glow. I glanced at him out of the corner of my eye and gasped when I saw him without horns, looking like a human. Slowly, I was starting to realize what was going on.

He was at least part siren and had been using spells to alter what he looked like to other people. He must have also been part mage to use the portals. That was why he felt like a hybrid, because he was one.

"Enough, I'm tired. I shall retire for the day. Perhaps, after you've had some sleep, you shall remember to show respect to your elders," he said and glared down at me. "Then, I will explain the powers you have and what I meant about being a goddess."

My elder, alright. He was likely a hybrid that had been part of the group that tried to take over Jinla and had fought against Nana Jolie and Great Aunt Leona. I really wished they were here right now. Or at least Dad, since he was part siren and resistant to their powers.

He left the room and I turned to Jol, my hair no longer glowing. "I apologize for any disrespect I may have shown to you. It was not my intention. Sometimes, this darkness ..." I raised the snake before making it disappear, curled back up inside of me, "... it causes me to be quick to talk instead of think."

"I appreciate your apology, but it is not necessary, as you did not disrespect me. Come, let me escort you to your room." He looked at the others in the room and said, "Hold off on enacting the plans we discussed today. I need to investigate a few things first."

They stood, bowed, and said, "Yes, Your Majesty."

Jol waved for me to follow him and I did with Dhun on my heels.

"Would you be able to take me outside?" I asked him. "Or somewhere that has soil?"

He stopped, spun, and frowned down at me. "Why?"

"I wanted to test a theory I had. You said I couldn't leave the castle with Dhun and Zoman, but couldn't you take me? I wouldn't need much time, just a few minutes."

Jol thought about it, his eyes narrowed as if I was trying to trick him. After a long moment, he sighed and nodded. "Fine, but you must stay close to me."

Walking so we were almost touching, I asked, "Is this close enough?"

His lips twitched up into a smile. "Yes, that will do."

He took me out a back door that opened to a little courtyard.

"This isn't part of the castle?" I asked.

"It used to be a garden," he said. "It used to be full of flowers and plant life," he answered.

So, why couldn't Dhun have taken me here then?

Almost immediately to answer my question, one of the bat-like demons flew overhead. When it spotted Jol, it flew in the opposite direction.

Walking out into the blackened dirt, I felt a deep sadness at all of the death. It hurt my soul to see so much nature devastated by whatever plague or curse had caused it.

There was a draw to a spot that felt like it used to be a

flower bush, similar to a rose bush back home. Getting down onto my knees, I pressed my hands into the soil, cringing at the acrid scent that filled my nostrils as I stirred it up. Closing my eyes, I tapped into my elven powers, my connection to nature, and reached down deep beneath the top layer, searching for signs of life. For any sign that it could be nurtured or grow.

The faintest pulse at least six feet down responded.

It was weak, but it was there!

"Can you pour some of my water that is in Dhun's pack onto the backs of my hands?" I requested, keeping my eyes closed to keep my connection.

"What are you hoping to do?" Zoman asked.

"Shush, don't interrupt her," Jol ordered. I felt him kneel beside me and the next moment the water dripped onto my hands.

Moving the water, I forced it down to the pulse I had felt. I surrounded that little bud of life with the water and sent some of my magic to it, nurturing it, coaxing, and begging it to grow.

It responded, but barely.

Darkness, it was surrounded by darkness. Light, it needed light!

"I need a shovel," I said urgently.

"What?" Jol asked.

"I need you to dig six feet below my hands," I ordered. "I can't move or I might lose it."

Dhun barked and started digging with his claws, flinging dirt so hard I heard it hitting the walls of the courtyard and the castle.

Jol squatted on my other side and dug with his hands as well. I was glad my eyes were closed, because watching the king dig with his bare hands would have caused me to cry.

"Your Majesty," Zoman gasped.

Jol didn't respond, just kept digging.

Another set of hands started digging in front of me, which meant Zoman was helping as well.

The pulse of life shifted as the dirt was dug and then it was in the light.

"Stop!" I ordered and all three males froze.

"I see it," Jol whispered, astonished. "A sprout."

Zoman whispered, "But the Grand Advisor said—"

"He said a lot of things, I'm sure," I whispered. "Come on, little sprout. You've got your light and your water. Show your king what you can do."

I swirled the water around it in a circle, letting it touch the roots without blocking the light or letting the water soak into the soil too much to lose it.

The sprout responded, doubling in size.

Zoman gasped.

My powers weakened, my abilities almost maxed out. I had to let it go. I had to let it try to thrive on its own.

"Little sprout, I have to let you go. You have to do this on your own for a bit. I'll soak the soil around you so you have water to grow. Don't die on us. Fight. You can do this."

"She's talking to a plant like it's a person," Zoman whispered, clearly thinking I was insane.

Pushing the water directly into the soil around the plant, I released my hold and opened my eyes. The little, dark green pair of leaves glowed in the early evening light.

"Go get water and one of the protective nets," Jol ordered Zoman.

Smiling, I turned to Jol, who stared at the plant as though it were the first time he'd seen one. "There is life, Jol. It needs help, but it is there."

He turned to me, eyes wide, and said, "You really are a goddess."

Shaking my head, I said, "I'm pretty weak when it comes to my nature magic. There are much stronger elves in my world."

Jol surprised me by leaning over and pressing his lips to mine. "You *are* a blessing, whether a goddess or princess or queen. And while the Grand Advisor may have misinterpreted some things from his visions or lied, you are the one I needed to come here."

FOUR

After the shock of Jol kissing me wore off, we went to the kitchen to make food, and he surprised me by inviting me to his room to share the meal. While I was slightly nervous about going to his room, uncertain if he had the wrong impression, my curiosity outweighed my nervousness. I hadn't seen his room yet, and I wondered what the mysterious demon king lived like compared to the guest room I was using.

His room turned out to have a living room, bedroom, and a patio that had a cover so you could sit outside even while it rained with a small round table. The outdoor set up was definitely one I wanted to mimic if I ever got a house of my own.

Walking around his room, I inspected the knickknacks he had on his dresser and shelves. They were all from my world and were random things like a ball, a dragon's scale, a radio, and a picture frame with a stock photo in it. There were also several small mana stones in the room.

"They're gifts from those who travel to your world," he explained when he saw me looking at the picture frame. "Things that intrigued them so they gave them to me. Come, let's eat before it gets cold."

Following him out to the balcony, I sat in the chair he pulled out for me and waited until he sat before picking up the fork to eat. I'd taken some of the items in his "cold box" as he called it and pantry and made a basic shepherd's pie. I had tasted it after cooking, so I knew it tasted good, but I waited for Jol to taste it first.

He took a bite, and his eyes widened. "This is delicious."

"Thank you," I said and ate my bite. "I'm not the best cook, but I try to learn new recipes that I know others will enjoy."

"I've never had anything like this. It's very flavorful." He took three big bites and closed his eyes as he ate.

I knew I was spoiled in comparison to others in my world, but seeing him enjoy a simple dish so much made my heart hurt for him and his people. There was so much I took for granted, even when I tried to be understanding.

"If we can come to a peaceful agreement, I would love to show you around the main city and take you to my favorite restaurants," I said. "My mom's favorite restaurant has the best dessert."

"Dessert?" he asked.

"Sweet treats," I answered. Tapping a finger against the necklace's gem as I looked out at the city view, I said, "I wonder if I could find a portal to go through and grab some stuff and come back like you send your troops?"

"You ... would come back?" he asked softly.

Looking back at him, I frowned and said, "Of course. I've been nothing but honest with you, Jol. I want to help you and your people."

"Only because we're threatening to take over your world," he countered.

I shook my head. "No, because I want to help. My goal has always been to help those less fortunate than me. I don't know what war the Grand Advisor told you about, but I don't think it needs to resort to that. I feel a sort of ... kinship with you and your people. As friends, we can help each other."

"Friends?" he asked and smiled softly. "I like the sound of that."

"Eat!" I said quickly. "We can talk boring politics and things later. Your food will get cold out here from the wind."

He gave me a soft smile and resumed eating.

Jol seemed like a kind male, so why wasn't he mated? I had no idea how old he was or what he had dealt with other the last decade.

"Jol, why aren't there very many female demons?"

His eyes widened. "Oh, there are. The females just prefer to live together in communities away from the city. They hunt together and raise their children together. They'll come to the city to find mates or buy items, but prefer to live their lives separately from the males."

"And none of these females caught your eye?" I asked and leaned my chin on my hand now that I'd finished eating.

"There was one," he admitted and a dark cloud seemed to settle over him, "but she was killed."

An uneasy feeling settled in the pit of my stomach as I guessed what he was going to say next.

"By one of your demon hunters."

"I'm so sorry," I whispered. "I can't imagine how painful that must have been."

"Death is part of life," he said and shrugged, but I could see the painful memory still lingered in the tenseness of his shoulders and the ways his eyes narrowed.

After he finished eating and we cleaned our dishes, I went back to the courtyard to check on the plant. Jol hadn't said I couldn't come back out here, and since it was part of the castle, I figured it was safe. Dhun had whined a bit, but followed me because he didn't want to leave me alone. Zoman was nowhere to be found, so I assumed that meant Jol felt I was safe enough without him as a continued guard.

The little plant with its two green leaves looked the same as when we'd left it and Zoman had added a chain link metal cage around it to keep birds and small animals from eating it.

Dhun walked around the courtyard, nose to the ground, snuffling loudly. Every now and then he would pause, tilt his head to the side, and start to dig a hole.

"What are you doing?" I asked after the third hole.

He stuck his snout into the hole, huffing loudly, looked back at me and barked.

I walked over and knelt to look in the hole, but there was nothing there. "I don't understand, Dhun. What do you want? What are you looking for?"

He ran over to the plant, nudged the cage gently, then ran back to the hole.

"Oh! You think there's a plant here?" Could he smell the plant?

Barking, he danced in a circle.

Setting my hands into the hole, I closed my eyes and tried to feel for life. Immediately, less than three inches below, I felt it. "You're right!" I shouted as my eyes flew open and I looked at Dhun. "There is life here! Can you smell them?"

He barked and bobbed his head.

"Dhun, I need water and more of those cages. Can you find Zoman or Jol and—"

"Well, what do we have here?" an unfamiliar voice said in a strange purring tone.

Looking up, I stared at the demon as I tried to figure it out. It had feline ears, a feline-human combination face, and a tail that was swishing back and forth behind it. It reminded me of Triston when he was in warrior shift, though his tiger stripes always showed and this demon's body was devoid of fur. The tail had short quills like Dhun's.

Dhun growled and stepped between the demon and I.

"Hello," I greeted as I stood and dusted off my hands. "I'm a guest of King Jolmach's."

It canted its head. "A guest? We don't have guests here. Not since the plague. I think you're a thief and I've caught you red handed in the King's Garden. The punishment for that is death, little thief." It leapt to the ground beside me and I realized their hands were feline paws with thick claws that reminded me of Triston and his cheetah paws.

"My name is Princess Liliana," I said with a smile. "What is your name?"

"Oh, the thief is a princess?" the demon said and laughed.

In a mocking tone, they bowed and said, "Then I shall be *Princess* Azgon." She laughed a tittering laugh. "Yes, yes! I like it. Princess Azgon."

Clearly, she was mocking me, but it was okay. I was an outsider here.

"It's nice to meet you, Princess Azgon."

She tittered and purred. "Well, the pleasure will be short lived since I have to kill you."

Dhun barked and growled at her.

She hissed at him. "Quiet, you traitor! We all know you were drafted to the other side while you stayed there!"

Dhun snarled and puffed up, his quills rattling in threat.

"Easy, there's no need for any of us to fight," I said and raised my hands.

"No fighting. Just your death," she said with a nonchalant shrug.

Sighing, I opened up my powers, summoning the darkness. "I don't want to fight you, but I'm not going to let you kill me, either."

Her eyes widened at the shadow snake wrapped around my arm. "You have shadow powers?"

"Among others," I said and shrugged one shoulder.

Azgon tapped a claw against her thigh, silent a moment, but then shrugged and said, "No matter. Thief must die." She leapt at me and Dhun headbutted her in the stomach, knocking her back from me. She spun, kicked him in the side, and sent him flying into the garden wall.

"Dhun!" I yelled, worried as he slumped unconscious to the ground. My hair began to glow as my fury over him being hurt grew.

Her claws sliced my arm open, making me hiss in pain and jump away. My shadow snake struck as she neared again, biting down on her arm and making her cry out in pain. She tried to pull it off, but since it was made of smoke, her hand simply passed through the spot she tried to touch. Clawing her own arm, she forced the snake to release her and return to me.

We both stood, squared off, arms bleeding, snarling at each other.

"What is the meaning of this?" Jol snapped, a force similar to an alpha command made me take a step back.

"Y-Your Majesty," Azgon said and bowed her head. "I-I caught this thief!"

"Thief? What could she be stealing from this dead garden, Azgon?" He stomped closer to us, brows furrowed and fury radiating throughout his body and making his aura red.

Azgon squatted, trying to make herself as small as possible.

Dhun got to his feet, shook his head, and trotted over to Jol.

"It's alright," I said, not knowing if he might kill her for hurting me. "It was a misunderstanding." My relief that Dhun was alright lifted a huge weight from my shoulders and my hair stopped glowing.

"Dhun told you she was a guest," Jol snapped, ignoring me. "Yet you dared to attack him *and* my guest?"

"Azgon is sorry, Your Majesty," she whispered, her back bowed as she moved farther away from both Jol and I. She glanced at me and said, "Her wound is healed already. See?

Azgon didn't cause too much damage. Just ... just trying to scare. No death."

"Tell everyone you know that this woman is under my protection and the punishment for harming her is death. Get out of my sight, Azgon, or I will declaw you," Jol threatened with a deep, vicious growl.

Azgon glanced at me one more time, this time with curiosity, before leaping up to the wall, and disappearing over it.

"Why didn't you summon me?" Jol asked as he inspected my arm.

"Huh?" I asked, trying to process what had just happened.

"The stone. I gave you the stone so you could communicate telepathically with me if you needed me. Why didn't you use it?"

Reaching into my pocket, I pulled it out and admitted, "I forgot about it. And I was trying to get her to understand that I wasn't a thief."

Sighing, he ran a hand through his hair, between his horns.

Were his horns sharp on the ends? They were pointed and looked sharp.

"What are you doing out here, anyway?"

"Oh!" I gasped, grabbed his hand, and dragged him to the new plant Dhun had found. "Dhun can smell them! I need more water and cages!"

His eyes widened as he looked from me to Dhun to the plant and back. "That's remarkable. But wait ... instead of growing these, we should be trying to grow crops. These are just flowers."

Heat flooded my cheeks in embarrassment. "Oh, I didn't know what they were. I'm sorry. I just got so excited that I—"

Jol set a hand on my cheek and said, "Little Queen, don't explain yourself."

More heat filled my face. "Jol, I—"

Dhun barked as Zoman ran into the garden.

"What happened? I saw Azgon fleeing with her tail tucked between her legs."

"She attacked our little queen. I let her go, knowing she would spread word quickly to the others not to mess with Lily."

Our little queen? I needed to explain to him that I basically already had mates. It wasn't official, but—

"Come, let's go back inside," I said. "I don't want to cause anymore misunderstandings."

Dhun whined, but complied.

"I'm going to go wash up," I informed them and showed my dirt covered hands.

Dhun started to follow, but I shook my head at him. "I'd prefer to shower alone."

"She's in the castle, so she'll be fine," Zoman reassured him. He looked at me and said, "Do not leave the castle, not even to the garden."

I saluted him mockingly. "Yes, sir."

He scowled and I smiled, proud of myself for irritating males no matter what world I was in.

Hurrying up the stairwell, I made it to the floor my guest

bedroom was on, but had to pull out my book to look at the floorplan diagram to turn down the correct hallway.

The Grand Advisor stepped out of a room just before my door and set his hand on my head. "You need an attitude adjustment, little *hybrid*."

He used some weird power that had sizzling pain shooting throughout my body, like being electrocuted, and I was unable to move. I couldn't even scream as I dropped to my knees before him.

CHAPTER
FIVE

"Are you alright?" Zoman asked.

I sat up, rubbing my head. "Wh-Where am I? What happened?"

"You came to take a shower, but when you didn't return for so long, King Jolmach asked me to check on you. We found you here in the hallway, on the floor."

"The last thing I remember was leaving you guys. I-I ..." Was there something else? Something else that happened? It felt like there was, but now I couldn't remember. It was a faint tingling memory, just outside of my ability to grasp it.

"Perhaps you should wait on the shower," Zoman said and helped me stand. "Come with me to the kitchen and we'll get your hands washed there."

"Okay," I agreed with a nod, but when I tried to walk, I felt dizzy and stumbled.

Zoman grabbed my arm, slung it around his shoulders, and put his arm around my waist. "Did you hit your head when you fainted or something?"

"Maybe," I said uncertainly. "I ... I don't know."

When we walked into the kitchen, Jol's eyes narrowed at Zoman holding me.

"I found her on the floor in the hallway outside her guest room," Zoman explained.

Jol walked over and inspected my head, forcing Zoman to back away from me. He gently pushed my hair away from my face along the hairline. "I don't see any wounds."

"I heal pretty fast," I said. "If I fell an hour ago, there would be no wound left, just dried blood."

"No dried blood either," he said and stepped back, scowling down at me.

I gripped the edge of the counter and said, "I just need a minute to regain my sense of balance."

"Here, drink some water," Zoman said and held out a cup for me.

"Thank you." I drained the entire cup in one gulp.

"Let me finish making food. Food will help," Jol said.

"Where's Dhun?" I asked. The pup was usually with us.

"He disappeared shortly after you left to shower," Jol admitted. His frown deepened, and he said, "Zoman, try to contact him and search the castle for him."

Jol finished making food, a dish of meat, carrots, and pota-toes. He held both our plates in his hand and asked, "Can you walk on your own?"

I nodded.

"You can hold my arm if you want," he said.

Sliding my hand through his arm, on the inside of his elbow, I walked silently beside him. This had never happened to me before. What could have caused me to faint and not remember?

"You seemed rather upset with the Grand Advisor earlier," Jol said after a moment. "Can you explain what caused your ire?"

"Upset? No, I'm not upset with him," I said and shook my head. "Just ... confused. I've been trying to figure out what this darkness is since it became part of me. He seems to know, and I just want to know what it is. To know how to deal with it and learn more about it."

"Do you truly have the ability to see the future?" he asked.

I nodded. "Though, with all visions, it's impossible to tell when that specific vision will come true. It could be hours or years."

His eyes widened. "Really?"

I nodded again. "I had a vision that came true an hour later and another one that came true one year later."

"The Grand Advisor seemed to believe his visions were going to come true soon."

We reached his room and sat on the patio again to eat.

"Each person has different powers and levels of powers. Perhaps he knows when his will happen. I do not know what he is capable of, though it seems he is very powerful." Something at the back of my mind was trying to come forward, but it felt blocked. "I hope to be able to talk to him again soon. To learn more from him."

Jol scowled and said nothing in reply.

"The family I was adopted into, there are a few who have visions, they are not able to tell when it will happen either.

Perhaps ... perhaps the battle he sees won't happen anytime soon. Perhaps, we, you and my family, could be allies. Perhaps it is your descendants who quarrel with mine?"

He gave no reply, but his brows seemed to furrow deeper, if that were possible.

We ate in silence and just as I finished, Jol straightened with a start and growled. "Come with me."

"What's wrong?" I asked.

"Zoman found Dhun. He's done something bad."

Dhun had done something bad? The pup seemed like he followed the rules as much as he could.

Jol lead us down to the garden where we found it destroyed, dug up and dirt flung everywhere.

My hands went to my mouth as I saw the sprout that I had started regrowing torn to pieces. Dropping to my knees, I felt tears fall down my face and onto the blackened dirt beneath. My hair glowed, a stark contrast to the bleakness before me.

It really was impossible. This world and its people would never be able to regrow crops. They were doomed.

"What have you done?" Jol roared at Dhun. His voice and anger caused the ground to quake.

Dhun cowered in the corner with his tail tucked between his legs and whined.

"What do you mean you don't remember? You don't remember destroying the sprout?" Jol demanded.

Dhun shook his head, whined, and curled up smaller.

"I don't believe you!" Jol bellowed. "Take him to the cells."

I wanted to object, but as I picked up one of the pieces of

the sprout, the words died on my tongue, and fresh tears sprouted.

"Come, let's go back inside. I don't know what's going on in this castle, but I intend to find out." Jol helped me to my feet and back into the castle. "You can use my bathroom to shower. I'll stay in the living room so you have your privacy, but I don't want you to be alone right now."

"Okay," I agreed with a nod, feeling numb at the death of the sprout and Dhun's behavior.

THE FOLLOWING DAY, the Grand Advisor returned to meet with me. Jol wanted to stay in the room, but I assured him it was okay. Reluctantly, he agreed to leave.

"You'll have to forgive him," I said softly, "we had an incident yesterday and it put him on edge."

"An incident?" the Grand Advisor asked with a scowl and stroked his beard.

"So, you said you would provide me more information on this power and what you meant about me being a goddess," I reminded him.

"What do you know about hybrids?" he asked.

I frowned. "Um, everything. Or at least everything that we know so far. My parents have been working hard to learn as much about our people as possible. How do you know about hybrids?"

"I've had the ability to see your world for a while now,"

he admitted. "I've been specifically following up on information about hybrids when our people go into your world. I have them grab newspapers and such."

That did make sense, but there seemed to be something else. Something at the edge of my mind ... *again*. Just out of reach.

"Hybrids are more powerful than full-blooded beings as they can combine their powers from the different races that they are born from," he explained. "The spell that was used against you, it seems to have contained bits from mages, sirens, and demons."

My eyes widened, and I gasped. "What?"

He nodded. "The darkness, the smoky power you use, is a demon power."

"Are you ..." I swallowed hard. "Are you insinuating that I am part demon?"

"Do you not feel a kinship to these people, myself included?" he asked with an arched brow.

I did, but I had thought perhaps there was something else...

"So, I am ... part demon?"

"It would seem so. Only a demon would be able to harness the power like you can."

Everything I thought I knew was crumbling around me. My parents ... my grandparents ... the trio ... would they care? Would they still love me, want to mate with me, once they found out?

"In fact, you bear a striking resemblance to someone I once knew, a former monarch here. I haven't mentioned it to King Jolmach, but I believe you are a princess."

"Wait, what? I am an adopted princess of the hybrids ..."

He shook his head, interrupting me. "I believe you are Princess of the Demons."

My ears rang and dizziness overtook me, forcing me to lean my head on the table before me and take shallow breaths. My hair glowed bright, casting rainbows around us.

"Princess? Princess?" Grand Advisor called.

"Air," I whispered. "I ... need air."

Panic attack. I was having another panic attack.

Arms picked me up and after a dizzying several seconds, I was back in the garden, set on the cool ground.

Digging my fingers into the burnt soil, I closed my eyes and grounded myself. Wind. I could feel the wind. Sun. I could feel the sunlight. Jol. I could smell Jol.

"Little Queen?" Jol asked.

"I apologize," the Grand Advisor said. "I think the information I provided her gave her quite a shock."

"What information?" Jol demanded with a growl.

"That she bears demonic blood and is in fact, Princess of the Demons," he answered.

Jol didn't respond and when I looked up at him, I saw disbelief on his face.

"She uses the Third to Reign's powers," the Grand Advisor went on. "You cannot deny that."

"You think ..." he swallowed. "You think she is a missing royal? A child raised not here, but in the other world and not taught about her demon heritage?"

"Yes," the Grand Advisor said with certainty. "I believe that's why you feel such a pull to her. Because you recognize she is of the royal bloodline and must be protected."

I wanted to argue, but within me, it felt ... *right*.

"Also, because she is an ideal potential mate for you now that you are king," the Grand Advisor added.

A potential mate to Jol? No, I had the trio. Jol seemed kind and caring, but my heart already belonged to Mason, Trey, and Kayden.

"You ..." I opened my eyes and looked up at the Grand Advisor. "You still didn't explain the goddess thing to me."

"Perhaps this is enough for the day. You clearly took the news about your heritage a bit harder than I anticipated. I will come back tomorrow, after you have had time to rest and digest the information." He bowed his head to Jol and then bowed his head to me.

My eyes widened and my heart pounded again.

Jol picked me up in a bridal carry, startling me. "Don't worry, even if he is wrong about your bloodline, I will still keep you safe while you're here. I was protecting you before it was mentioned you might be part demon."

"If he's right ... I'm not sure what that will mean for my place back home." Would my parents have to revoke my status as Princess of the Hybrids?

Would the rest of my family view me differently? Would the trio view me negatively? Would they no longer want to court me? Too many questions without any answers. It was maddening. *Maddening*.

"You're stressing a lot about this. Is it because you think we're evil?" His voice was soft and he tried to look uninterested, but I could sense a bit of worry. His aura had been swirling chaotically ever since Grand Advisor's announcement.

"No, it's not because I think you're evil," I answered honestly. "But this ... *complicates* things significantly in my world."

"With the ones courting you?"

"Among others," I murmured.

"Well, if you are part demon, as it seems, you are now with your people and it makes the protective feeling I have for you understandable."

I wasn't sure what to say to that. Especially since Jol's goal was to go to my current world and take it over.

"Why would the protective feeling be understandable now?" I asked curiously.

"Because, before I was king, I was a royal guard for the monarchs and swore a blood oath to protect the royal bloodline. That desire to guard the royal bloodline still courses through me, but sadly, they are all gone."

"Wait, you aren't from the royal bloodline?"

Shaking his head, he pushed open the door to my guest bedroom and set me on the chaise lounge.

"During the battle, one traitor assassinated many of the royals. Most of the royal guard were murdered as well. I almost lost my life, but survived and took my revenge on the traitor. The people gave me the title of king and I've been in that position ever since."

"That had to have been rough," I said and patted his hand where it lay on the chaise lounge arm. "I'm sorry."

"Is there anything I can get you?"

"No, I just need to rest and think."

He pulled out a stone from his pocket, the one he'd used previously to call for Zoman, and set it on the side table next to me. "If you need me or need anything, hold this stone in your hand, picture me, and talk. I'll hear."

"Okay," I agreed.

He looked at me with an odd expression, then turned, and left, shutting the door behind him.

Laying down, I closed my eyes and took big, deep breaths.

Were they right? Was I part demon?

Was that why I felt something to the demons that I had thought was because they were hybrids?

Summoning my power, I looked at the snake and asked, "Are you demonic power? Or are you something else?"

The smoke snake's tongue darted out as it tasted the air, but it gave me no answer.

With a sigh, I dismissed the power and threw my arm over my eyes. How had things become more complicated in just a day? One single day!

CHAPTER
SIX

After half a day of moping, I vowed to move on and continue with my quest to learn more about this world and its people.

With a bit of begging, I convinced Jol to release Dhun so that I could take him with me to explore. Jol didn't like the idea of me exploring outside of the castle, but Zoman agreed to go with us and vowed to protect me. Even then, it took a bit more begging and some use of my ultra-adorable pout to break his resolve.

Bag packed with snacks and water, and me wearing a new set of clothes courtesy of Zoman's brother's mate, the three of us headed out into the city.

Unlike in the castle, Zoman stayed next to me.

He walked on my right while Dhun walked on my left.

The demons who walked about the city eyed me warily, but one look from Zoman sent them scurrying on their way.

Most of the buildings were housing of one kind or another, apartments, duplexes, and houses, but there were a couple stores as well. We walked into one store and I was immediately intrigued by all the items. They were pieces of the burned trees, carved into shapes with symbols on them.

"What are these?" I asked Zoman.

"Totems with protective symbols," he answered. Pointing to one he said, "This is a symbol for strength." Pointing to another, he said, "This is one for increased stamina."

"Do they work, or are they just for decoration?"

"How rude!" the male storekeeper shouted. He was a large demon, his head and horns were so tall he had to duck in the shop to keep his horns from getting stuck in the ceiling. He was wide as well, his shirt buttons were strained as they tried to keep from snapping off, bits of his skin and ... fur ... showing through the gaping holes.

"Rude?" I asked.

He snorted. "I do not sell fakes! These are one hundred percent legitimate protection symbols."

"She's not from here," Zoman told him. "She doesn't know about our world and is learning."

The storekeeper narrowed his eyes at me. "You have no horns?"

"I'm only part demon," I explained. Just saying it made my heart pound, and yet, I also felt a strange sense of right-ness to acknowledge it.

"You poor thing," he whispered and shook his head sadly.

Apparently, it was important to them to have horns. I wondered if the shape or size mattered to them?

"Do I have to hold them or just keep them in a pocket to work?" I picked up the figure that looked a bit like Jol, it even had a spiked mace in its hand, with the symbol for strength on it.

"You put it on your mantle, recite the words, and it will activate. Then, you leave it on your mantle and it will increase your strength, including your resolve," the storekeeper explained. His voice was much softer and his body had relaxed now that he'd learned I wasn't insulting him.

"Will it strengthen just me or everyone who lives in the house?"

"One item per person," he explained.

"What are these symbols for?" I asked and moved to the next shelf.

The storekeeper explained them one by one to me. I pulled out my notebook and tried to draw the first symbol, but the storekeeper snatched the book out of my hand and the pencil.

"Hey!" I shouted.

He waved his hand dismissively. "Go look around more. I'll draw them for you. Your first attempt hurts my soul."

My mouth dropped. "Now who is being rude?"

Zoman chuckled, but covered his mouth when I turned to him.

Going to the next row of shelves, I inspected the other items offered for sale. There were some cute items and I wished I had money or items to trade for some of the things.

As I turned to the next shelf, my eyes widened, and I gasped at the item I saw. Reaching out a shaky hand to pick up the silver snake with ruby-colored eyes wrapped around a lily, I stroked a finger down it, feeling a deep pull to it.

"What have you found?" the shopkeeper asked as he stomped over to me.

"What is this?" I asked and held it on my palm so he could see it.

"Ah, that. It's from an old prophecy."

A strange anxiousness filled me. "What does the prophecy say?"

He held up a claw-tipped finger, walked behind the counter, and grabbed a book. He paused and said, "You must swear to tell no one that I, a male, have a book."

That seemed a bit odd, but I nodded and said, "I swear."

Zoman dipped his head.

The storekeeper opened the book and read, "In the realm where demons dance and death looms, in a time when darkness threatens to eclipse the light, a savior shall emerge as a ruby-eyed serpent with sparkling silver scales, born of mystic origins. Within the serpent's gaze, a flicker of crimson defiance against the usurper will weave salvation and life into the fading realm through a harmonious dance of serpentine and floral grace. Upon the eve of despair, when the moon ascends to its zenith, the serpent, bathed in ethereal radiance, will sacrifice all to save the worlds. The savior's sacrifice will bloom into a silver lily as a testament to the power of love in the face of darkness."

My hair began to glow, but I took shallow breaths to calm myself and stop its glow.

Was I just being conceited to think that the prophecy sounded like it could be about me? I was a ruby-eyed serpent with white scales. And my origins were definitely unique, even amongst the hybrids back home.

"Can ... can I copy that down?" I asked.

The storekeeper looked around nervously. "Don't let the

Grand Advisor see it. This is from the Third to Reign's time and we aren't supposed to keep items like this."

I made an x over my heart and said, "I promise I won't tell."

After another moment of hesitation, he slid the book towards me and my notebook where he'd drawn the symbols and their meanings.

Quickly, I copied down the words, being sure to copy it exactly, word for word.

"Thank you," I said and put the book into Dhun's bag.

"Take these," the shopkeeper said and held out the serpent and the strength totem.

"I don't have any money or anything to barter," I said quickly.

"You're the first to show such interest in a long time, and all demons should have at least one totem. Consider it a welcome gift." He smiled, showing off serrated, triangular teeth.

"Thank you," I said and clutched them to my chest.

Zoman held open the door for me and we went to another store.

After looking at the other three stores, we sat on what used to be a fountain, but was empty of water and filled with ash. I pulled out a granola bar that I'd found in the kitchen and ate it.

Even the fountain here had mana stones. What did they use them for? They seemed to be placed all over. They weren't being used as a barrier that I could tell. It seemed strange to have so many mana stones not in use.

"Do you believe in prophecies?" I asked Zoman, while watching the demons around us.

Many were curious about me, openly staring, though from a distance.

"Prophecies do have a tendency to come true, but I *hate* how convoluted they often are. They'll talk about a flower, but it's actually a power or something crazy like that," Zoman answered.

Dhun snorted in agreement.

"Hmm," I whispered.

A thought occurred to me.

"Do you have magic users?"

Zoman scoffed. "Of course we do. What do you take us for?"

"Why haven't I seen any?" I asked. "The only demons I've yet to see are fighters."

"You have only seen a few of our kind," he replied. "We're spread out all over our world, waiting for portals to open, to go and find supplies, and bring them back."

"What type of powers do you guys have? Elemental?"

"Some have elemental," he answered with a nod. "Fire powers are the most common." He paused and looked at me. "Though, none have powers to grow or nourish plants like you do."

Why would they have elemental powers, but no plant powers? That seemed odd. Since they didn't differentiate themselves by races, like we did, I couldn't be sure of the answer to my next question.

"Are there certain demons capable of it? Ones that look a certain way?"

"Oh yes, the ones that look ..." he stopped talking and scoffed. "You're just trying to get information out of me! Sneaky woman."

"What? I'm not asking for malicious reasons," I said, though, it would be helpful for my family to know which demons to watch out for if they did go to battle.

"Tsk. You're just like the others, conniving!" Zoman got to his feet angrily and turned away. "I'll wait over here until you are ready to leave."

Dhun whined and set his head on my knee.

I stroked his quills carefully and asked, "You know I wasn't asking for malicious reasons, right?"

He whined again and closed his eyes as I continued to pet him.

A small demon child noticed us and ran over. "Your skin is so weird!" he shouted and poked my bare arm.

The child had small, thick horns at the top of his head, long, thick fangs like a vampire, and a tail that swished wildly behind him. His skin was covered in scales, similar to that of a dragon.

"Is it?" I asked, and let my snake scales flow over me. "Look again."

He looked down and gasped. "Scales! Like me! Wow, lady, you're super weird!" He laughed and the sound was so joyful that I found myself laughing with him.

"What's your name?" I asked.

"I'm Elrith!" he shouted.

"And what is your dream?"

He flexed his arms, though little muscle moved, and said, "I'm going to be a great warrior, like our king!"

Smiling, I patted his head between his horns and said, "I'm sure you will be. Where are your parents?"

He looked down. "They are dead, lady."

An orphan?

"Do you have no one to take care of you?"

He shook his head, but quickly looked up and smiled. "I can take care of myself! I don't need anyone."

My heart hurt to see the orphan boy, but I also knew so little about this place that I couldn't provide a way to help him. "Are you eating well?"

He nodded vigorously. "We have soup and bread most days at the town center."

Like a soup kitchen back home?

"I'm glad to hear that," I admitted.

He frowned. "You must not be from this area." His eyes narrowed on my hair. "And you have no horns? You must be picked on a lot." This time, he patted my head. "You poor thing."

The urge to laugh was high, but I held it in. "Yes, I am hornless, a truly sad occurrence."

"If you become a strong fighter, you can prove yourself worthy and get many mates!" he said with conviction. "You should do your best to help the demons."

Do my best to help the demons ...

If only life were that simple.

"I will try," I said and smiled, though my smile was a bit forced.

"I have to go. Be strong, lady!" The boy patted my hand and ran off across the city.

"You like kids?" Zoman asked.

"I was an orphan," I explained. "In my world, I help as many orphans as I can."

"That is commendable," Zoman said softly.

Dhun whined and yipped and Zoman nodded.

"What?" I asked.

"He said we should return to the castle since it is getting late and I agree. We mustn't worry the king needlessly."

"Okay," I agreed and stood. "Will you take me to other cities? To visit the women communities?"

"If our King allows it, yes," Zoman said and dipped his head to me. "As a demon, you should learn as much as you can about your people."

"Exactly," I said with a nod. "Now that I'm here and know my lineage, I want to absorb as much as I can."

"I'm still watching you," he muttered, but his face softened as he added, "but there is much you can learn about our ways without it being possibly detrimental should it get back to your world."

"I appreciate your loyalty to your people and your willingness to teach me as much as you can." I said and dipped my head to him.

He tsked. "Don't bow your head to me. You're a princess."

"And you are a loyal guard," I said back. "You deserve respect as well."

He didn't reply, but I noticed him walking a bit taller as we returned to the castle.

CHAPTER
SEVEN

After a bit of begging, we finally got permission from Jol to visit one of the nearby women's communities.

It took us an hour to get to the closest one, and the journey was pretty silent, but it was still pleasant. Part of me felt bad for enjoying my time here, but with no portals showing up, I had little hope of returning to my world anyway.

My best option was to record everything about this world that I could to hopefully get it to my family back home.

My notes had yet to mention my suspected demon ancestry. I just couldn't bring myself to write it down. Perhaps, if I delivered that blow to my family in person, it would be easier to absorb and they might take it better.

Though, the trio, I had no idea what to expect of our famed "Demon Hunters" when they discovered that I was part demon.

"You're scowling a lot. Do you need to rest?" Zoman asked, clearly concerned.

"No, I'm fine. I'm just trying to absorb everything I've learned so far and determine what I might want to learn still. It's hard to know what questions to ask when you don't know about the culture or the people."

He nodded. "That's understandable. Per our King's orders, I will provide you as much knowledge as I have. Though, the women will be better at providing you that information. They have many books and verbal stories that they pass down through their generations."

The village came into sight and several large female demons came out to greet us.

Most were not humanoid in shape, many had long horns and thick, leathery skin. A few had scales and wings as well as tails.

Several small children and females carrying babies had come out as well.

"What brings the King's guard here?" one of them asked.

"Princess Liliana Rubyserpent has been sent here to learn more about demons, per the order of King Jolmach," Zoman announced loud enough that all could hear.

Many whispered in surprise.

"You're a demon princess?" one of the demons with wings asked and scoffed. "You don't even have horns."

"I am part demon," I explained. "And sadly, I do not have horns."

"You've not been raised here?" an older female who shuffled forward with her back slightly stooped asked.

I shook my head. "It appears my parents snuck me away to the other world without the others knowing. I was raised there, and they did not tell me of my demon heritage."

"You don't remember your parents?" one of the children asked as he clung to the pants of the female beside him.

"I do not," I replied. "My mother died when I was very young and my father was killed when I was only four-years-old. I was adopted by the King and Queen of the Hybrids and raised by them under the assumption that I was a hybrid."

One of the females with a hunch at the top of her back, hobbled forward and clutched one of my hands in both of hers. "You poor thing! That must have been awful. Please, come sit at my fire and let us tell you about your people. Your *true* people."

A few of the females continued to glare at me, one even held a sword in her hand, but some looked at me with pitying expressions. The children were incredibly curious and followed us to a large firepit.

"Do you have another form?" the female with the hunched back asked me.

I nodded. "It's ... sometimes it scares people, especially children."

"Please, show us," she said. "It will help me in providing you some answers and advice."

Stepping back, I closed my eyes and shifted into my full snake form, curled up slightly so I didn't stretch across the area. As soon as I shifted, I felt ... different. Normally when I shifted into my snake form, it felt good, but as I shifted here, it felt *so much* better, like I was stronger here. Like my form was meant to be here.

"A ruby-eyed serpent not just in name?" the older female gasped and lifted shaking hands up to her mouth. I hadn't noticed until she did that, that she had sharp, pointed teeth.

Several of the other females, and all of the children, came closer, a few dropped to their knees as they faced me.

"It can't be," Zoman whispered as he stepped forward.

Four females stepped between us, hissing and growling at Zoman. Protecting me!

He raised his hands in surrender. "I wasn't going to harm the princess. I'm assigned to protect her, remember?"

"Stay away from her," the female who had asked me to shift snapped. Turning to me, she said, "You may shift back now, dear."

Reluctantly, I shifted back. It was easiest to speak in human form, but it had felt so good to be in my snake form.

"You truly are our missing princess," one of the females with silver fur and long, canine ears that flopped down to her shoulders whispered.

"How are you so certain?" I asked.

The hunched back female sat beside me and waved her hand at one of the others.

That female she'd waved at ran into a nearby house and returned shortly with a thick book with pages worn from use and discolored from age. She handed it to the hunched back female seated beside me, bowed, and hurried back several steps.

"Please give us space," she said to Zoman.

He scowled. "I am to protect the princess."

"None here will harm her and you are not of our community. You are lucky we allow you here even now. Go," she snapped.

To my surprise, Zoman bowed and walked to the fence that marked the edge of the city.

"This is our history book," she explained as she opened it once Zoman was gone.

"Skip forward, Nana Druth," one of the children said. "Don't tell her the boring stuff."

The hunched back female, Druth, hissed at the child, but flipped past several pages. She paused on one page, a painting of a beautiful female demon with thick, curved horns, and a long, thick tail that reminded me of a snake.

"This was the Third to Reign," she whispered and stroked a finger down the page. "She was exceptional in all ways. And she was the one who delivered the prophecies."

"Do you have many prophecies?" I asked.

She shook her head. "Only four; and three of those have already come to pass. Third to Reign had amazing premonition abilities." Lowering her voice, she whispered, "Even better than the Grand Advisor's."

"What was the fourth prophecy?" I asked.

She repeated the same prophecy that the storekeeper had told me, the same one I had recorded in my book, except for one additional line at the end. "Yet she will not reign and will pass the throne to a warrior of renown."

Opening my book, I wrote the phrase down.

The females gasped.

"You record in a book?" one whisper-hissed.

"It's a very common practice among my people," I said. "Do you not all do the same?"

"Here, it is mainly the females who record history on

paper. The males, they only care for the battle histories," the silver-furred female said and rolled her eyes.

"Grand Advisor does not like the recorded histories. He has tried many times to ban them, but so far King Jolmach has convinced him not to continue with that path," Druth said. "Plus, we are very good at hiding our books just in case he tries to come and take them."

Why would he want the histories destroyed?

"May I see your book? I can add some additional notes into it," one of the women asked.

"Sure," I said and held it out to her. This seemed the best place to get information on this world.

"Do you truly believe your prophecies?" I asked.

Druth held the history book to her chest and said, "We do not doubt the Third to Reign. She has proven true three out of four times and seeing you now, I believe her final prophecy is about to come true."

My throat tightened, and it became very hard to swallow.

"Tell me more," I requested.

Immediately, all the females gathered around, giving me information about their world, insights into their living situations, and a glimpse into a past that both surprised and saddened me.

They had moved to separate towns to raise their kids to reduce the number of attacks on the children. As their food sources continued to decrease over the years, the number of desperate demons willing to eat anything, including their own kind, increased.

I needed to find a way to help them. To fix this world

with its own heartache and people. A world of beauty even in a sea of death.

As they continued to provide information, one word caught my ears, "goddess." I turned to the demon female who had said it, the silver-furred, floppy-eared female who was writing in my book, and immediately put it together.

"You," I whispered.

She smiled sheepishly. "Yes, it was me who guided you that day. I have a rare ability to feel when a fellow demon female is in danger."

So, the Grand Advisor had lied! He hadn't been the one to talk to me and that was why he refused to speak to me about the goddess matter altogether!

"What does a goddess mean to you?"

"A powerful magic user, like the Third to Reign," she answered. "And, after our talks, I am certain you are her descendent. And that you are the prophesized one."

All who were gathered gasped and murmured to each other.

"A descendent of the Third to Reign?" one of the females asked. "Are you sure?"

She nodded and her ears flopped about. "Without a doubt. She uses the shadow powers that are passed down through the Third to Reign's lineage only."

"Then you would have been the heir to the throne, had your family not snuck you away," Druth whispered. Her eyes widened. "You cannot let Grand Advisor find out you are her descendent."

"What? Why not?" I asked.

They all looked at each other nervously, but seemed unwilling to say more.

"Can we teach you a dance?" the silver-furred demon asked me as she slipped the book back into my bag. She had written on several different pages.

"A dance?" I asked as she gently gripped my fingers with fur covered hands and helped me to my feet.

She nodded, and her canine-like ears flopped around. "It's one that all females are taught once they reach puberty. We perform it for the ones we wish to mate with."

My eyes widened, and I nodded quickly. "Yes, please!"

She smiled and led me over to the fire that they started as the sun had begun to set. "It's not too hard, so I bet you will pick it up in no time."

After watching the dance a few times, they showed me step by step, slowly, until finally, after an hour, I had the steps down.

"There you go!" the silver-furred female praised. "Keep practicing and you'll learn to do it faster and faster until you're ready to show the ones you want as mates."

"It's late, Lily. We should head back," Zoman said. "We were supposed to be back by nightfall, but you were having too much fun and I didn't want to interrupt you learning your dance."

"You're welcome back here, anytime," Druth said. She handed me my bag and whispered, "There is more written now in your book. More about the power you possess."

"Thank you," I whispered back and clutched the bag to my chest.

The silver-furred female took my hands gently in her

paws and said, "My name is Talrinir. I hope you visit us again."

"I will try," I promised. "Thank you, Talrinir."

As she pulled her hand back, I realized that she had left a small folded note in my hand. Quickly, I closed my hand into a fist and stuck it into my pocket to hide. I wasn't sure what the note said or why she felt the need to hide it from Zoman and Dhun, but I assumed it was important.

I said goodbye to everyone and hurried to catch up to Dhun and Zoman, who were at the edge of the town already.

"Thank you for bringing me here today," I said and smiled at both of them.

Dhun wagged his tail and Zoman returned my smile.

The trip back to the castle was pretty uneventful, there were a few times that demons started to get close to us, but immediately turned away when they realized it was Zoman with me.

Back in my room, I pulled out the piece of paper and gaped at the words written.

YOU MUST LEAVE this world before Grand Advisor realizes who you are and kills you.

Come see me in three days.

~T

HEART POUNDING, I sat on the chaise lounge and reread the two sentences a dozen more times.

Two knocks at the door made me yelp. I shoved the paper

into my mouth and quickly swallowed it. I almost choked and had to chug some water before I asked, "Who is it?"

"It's Zoman. King Jolmach has asked me to come escort you to his room. He would like to eat dinner with you."

"Okay, I'll be right out," I called back as I tried to calm my racing heart.

CHAPTER
EIGHT

Lying in the garden in my snake form, I enjoyed the warm sunlight along my scales and tried to figure out why I had such an uneasy feeling in my stomach.

Dhun lay near me, his eyes open as he kept guard. Zoman sat in the shade, humming a song that sounded familiar, though I couldn't place where I knew it from.

Yesterday, the Grand Advisor had come to see me, but when I brought up the "goddess" issue, he had gotten mad and then, strangely, I couldn't remember much of what we talked about after that. It was even more strange since Zoman claimed we had been in the conference room for over an hour and the Grand Advisor had come out very upset. So upset that he had stormed out of the castle without speaking to Jol or anyone else.

The more time I spent with the Grand Advisor, the less afraid of him I became. He was clearly trying his best to help the people here, though his abilities were limited since he could not help the land or grow things.

I felt the energy shift seconds before someone jumped over the wall, startling Dhun and Zoman to their feet.

"Lily!" a familiar female voice exclaimed.

I shifted to my human form and opened my eyes to find Talrinir squatted before me. Blood dripped down her head, one floppy ear completely coated in blood, and there were cuts all over her arms.

"Talrinir! What happened?" I gasped as I stood and hurried to examine her.

"He knows," she hissed. "He figured out I knew about you and sent his minions to try to kill me. It's not safe, you need to go. You need to return to your world."

"Wait, slow down. What are you talking about?"

"Who knows what?" Zoman demanded as he came up behind me.

She searched my face a moment, brows furrowed, then her eyes widened and she asked, "Did the Grand Advisor come to see you recently?"

"Yes, I met with him yesterday."

"What did you tell him?" She gripped my arms hard, her claws against my skin, but not piercing. "Princess, what did you tell him?"

"I—I don't know. I don't remember much of yesterday, to be honest."

She growled and said something in a language I didn't understand.

"Talrinir, what is going on?" Zoman snapped.

"He's erased her memory," she whispered and cupped my face. "If I'm right, Grand Advisor now knows that you're the prophesized one, what your lineage is, and you are in grave danger. I don't know why he hasn't killed you already, but you threaten everything he's done. Come with me now and I'll—"

"You're not taking her anywhere," Jol growled as he approached us. His aura was dark, billowing around him like a storm.

Talrinir dropped into a low bow, her head on the ground. "Your Majesty."

"Talrinir, why do you think he's going to hurt me?" I asked, ignoring Jol for the moment.

"He's not who he seems. He isn't a demon," she whispered. "You threaten to reveal his true identity and to take away everything he's spent the last decade building."

"How do you know about this?" Jol asked.

"We females spend our time on the edges of demon society. We watch many things happen that those within the walls don't see. I think ..." she swallowed hard, "... I think he has been brainwashing people and taking or overwriting their memories." She looked at me and asked, "Do you remember the note I gave you?"

My brows furrowed. "Note? What note?"

She whined. "It's as I feared. I gave you a note, told you that you were in danger and to meet me today. When I was attacked, I knew I had to come find you."

"You are making a lot of serious accusations," Jol said. "What proof do you have?"

"I do not have any proof. It's impossible to have proof when he changes people's memories and destroys history books."

Some part of me felt like she was telling the truth. Some

part of my mind, in the dark recesses, felt like I was forgetting something important and that she was right.

"I believe you," I said and gripped her paws, pulling her upright. "But it is impossible for me to leave without a portal, and the portals are random."

My hair glowed as fury over her being attacked because of me grew. Why was he doing this? What was his motivation? What did he hope to gain?

No, the portals were not random. Some memory, some knowledge that had been shoved to the back of my mind, struggled through a barrier and into the light.

Gasping, I said, "It's him. He creates the portals."

"What?" Jol asked.

Talrinir's eyes widened. "That makes sense. I don't know why I didn't see it before."

A guard ran into the garden and whispered urgently into Zoman's ear. Zoman jerked back after hearing what the guard had to say, then both ran out of the garden.

If she was right and the Grand Advisor had altered my memory or messed with my mind, it was possible for me to reverse it. If it was a siren ability he had used, Dad had taught me a few tricks.

Closing my eyes, I pictured my mind, pictured the wall I normally kept up around it, to protect myself from siren attacks.

When I realized the wall was completely gone, I knew Talrinir was telling the truth. To remove the tainted magic within, it would cause me a lot of pain, but I had to do it.

"I might faint, so I'm going to sit down," I said as I sat cross-legged next to Talrinir.

"What are you doing?" Jol asked, concerned.

"She's right, there's magic in my mind, a dark magic that's altered my mind in some way. I'm going to burn it out, and it's going to hurt."

"You can sense it?" she gasped.

I nodded. "My protective walls within my mind are destroyed."

Jol growled. "You're certain it's the Grand Advisor."

"Yes, it has his aura," I admitted once I realized it.

Jol growled again.

Taking a deep breath, I used the spell Mom had taught me, a mental fire flash to burn away siren magic.

The pain was so immense that I screamed and fell backwards.

Talrinir threw her arms behind mine so that I fell into her instead of on the ground. "I've got you."

There was so much in my mind. So much manipulation.

"I have to do it again," I panted. "There's … so much."

"I will hold you while you do it," she promised, "and try to provide you some comfort."

Using the spell again, I finally cleared away all of it and all of my true memories returned, making me gasp in disbelief. How had I forgotten so much?

Racing up to my room, I grabbed the bag that Dhun normally carried that contained my book, the protection charm I had been given by the shopkeeper, and reached beneath the bed where I had hidden the necklace, wrapped in a towel. I had forgotten about doing that a few days ago, but with all my memories back, I recalled that this necklace was most likely something that the Grand Advisor used to listen in on what I was doing or see who I was talking to. It was also likely how he created portals that I could use. Well, that was my working theory, anyway.

I returned to the garden at the same time as Zoman.

"There's news I must update you on," Zoman said urgently. His eyes darted to mine before he looked back at Jol and refused to look at me again.

"Go on," Jol said.

"This should be given privately," Zoman whispered, his stance rigid.

What would he not want to say in front of me?

"Is it my family?" I asked, standing and moving towards him. "Did my family go through a portal? Are they here?"

"Out with it," Jol ordered Zoman.

"The three demon hunters ... they're headed here from the east," Zoman admitted.

I gasped and Jol glanced at me with a frown.

"The one ..." Zoman swallowed hard. "The one you've been after is among them."

Jol growled deep in his chest. "Get my armor ready."

"Wait!" I snapped and grabbed his arm. "Wait, please. If it is who I think it is, they're my friends, the ones I'm cour—"

"The one who took my to-be mate is among them, and his death must be at my hand," Jol snarled.

"I understand it hurt you immensely to lose her. I can't bring her back, but killing him won't bring her back, either. Please, please don't go after them. He's my friend. He's ... they're my courters."

His brows rose in shock.

"This can all be fixed. We can come to a peace agreement

and we can help each other. But only if you give up on revenge. Please, Jol ..."

Zoman growled.

For the first time in my life, I bowed my head to another monarch. "Please, King Jolmach. I am begging you to spare his life. We didn't know your people were sentient. Please! I —I ... I love them!"

Jol staggered back a step as though I had physically struck him.

Talrinir and Dhun looked between Jol and I, but stayed silent.

"Your Majesty?" Zoman asked.

Jol's face hardened. "Fetch my armor, Zoman." He turned on his heel and headed towards the castle.

My legs gave out and I dropped to my knees. "No," I whispered. If Jol faced off against the trio, I wasn't sure who would survive, if any. If he killed one of them ...

Getting to my feet, I clenched my hands into fists at my side and shouted at his retreating back, "If you kill them, I won't help you! I won't help your plants or your people. Don't do this, Jol. Think of your people. We can work this out. We can be partners and restore your world."

Jol continued walking away, ignoring me.

Dhun crouched by me, whining softly.

I couldn't let this happen. I had to get the guys and leave. I had to prevent them from killing each other.

Putting the bag around my shoulders, I turned to Dhun, set my hand atop his head, and said, "I'm sorry, Dhun. I'm sorry it came to this. Tell Jol ..." I swallowed hard. "Tell him that we can still become allies. We can reach an agreement that will prevent war and save both of our worlds. Tell him I promise to find a way to save this world that doesn't require a battle."

Dhun whined and canted his head.

Pressing my lips against his snout I whispered, "Stay safe, friend."

Turning to Talrinir, I said, "You are in danger because of me. Come with me and you can live in my world. I will give you a safe place to live."

She shook her head. "I cannot. I must stay here to help as many as I can."

I bowed and said, "I will not forget your friendship."

Spinning around, I leapt up the wall, caught the top and pulled myself up and over it.

Dhun barked and whined, trying to come after me, but he couldn't. Talrinir called after me as well, but I ignored them both.

Taking off at a sprint, I headed east, praying to every god or goddess in existence to help me save my friends.

CHAPTER
NINE

After an hour of running, I came to Talrinir's small village, where a dozen or so females huddled together in the middle, children crying and encircled by them.

Their terror was evident, and I knew it had to be the trio.

As I ran by the females, I had to slide to a stop before running right into Trey in his dragon warrior form.

"Trey!" I screeched.

Kayden suddenly gripped my shoulders and kept me upright. "Lily? Is that really you?" he asked, pulled me forward to smell me, and wrapped his arms around me in a bone-crunching hug.

I shoved his chest. "Now's not the time for that. We need to leave. Now!"

One of the females snapped and asked, "What do you want?"

Turning, I held my hands up placatingly. "I'm sorry they scared you. We're leaving. You don't have to worry. You and the children are safe."

"They talk?" Trey asked, having shifted to human form.

"I have a lot to tell you, but we can't do that here. We—"

Trey pulled me into his arms and crushed his lips against mine. He pulled back and I noticed the short beard along his jaw. Resting his hand against my cheek he whispered, "Lily, we've been going mad trying to find you."

"I'm fine," I whispered, and patted his arm. "Now, where's Mason? We—"

The male in question pulled me out of Trey's hold, a hand on each of my arms, and shook me. "What were you thinking?" he shouted. He also had a beard, making it three for three. It wasn't a look I was used to, but it was one I definitely didn't hate.

"What?" I gasped as I pushed at his chest. "What are you talking about?"

"You went with them. You—"

"I was teleported!" I shouted to get him to stop. "I didn't come here willingly."

His body tensed a moment and then he staggered forward a step and hugged me, his nose against my neck. "I thought you were dead."

"We really don't have time, guys! We can have our tearful reunion later. We have to leave!"

"We can't leave without a portal," Trey reminded me.

"I know, but we need to head in that direction," I said and pointed to the north.

"Why that way?" Kayden asked.

"Because their king is headed this way from the west," I explained. Grabbing Mason's hand, I tugged and said, "Let's go. I'll explain on the way." I gave the females one more look, but Druth just nodded and made a shooing motion with her hand.

Thankfully, the guys stopped fighting me and we ran north.

"Here," I said and shoved the book into Kayden's hands. "I wrote down as much information as I could. We've been wrong about everything. Everything! They aren't violent, mindless creatures. They have their own society. They are wonderful, intelligent people with a civilization and culture of their own. They're just trying to survive and the people that come through don't always know how to speak. We've been killing innocent creatures without realizing it."

"This is a lot of information," Kayden whispered as he flipped through the book. "Wait, they have a king?"

"Yes, and one of you killed his to-be mate. He's after you all to kill whichever one of you did it." I glanced at Mason, who still held my hand. "I—I think it might have been you."

Mason shrugged, unworried and said, "I've killed a lot of them."

"What do you mean they're trying to survive?" Trey asked.

I had to slow down, my heart pounded and lungs burned from running to them and continuing to run. "Haven't you noticed the burnt land? There was a war and a plague and it wiped out their crops. They've been coming to our world to get resources and food to survive. There's also this advisor ... I will talk about him later, but he's told them that to survive they have to go to war with us, but I've been trying to convince Jol—"

"Who's Jol?" Mason asked, a bit of growl in his tone.

"King Jolmach, their king," I explained.

That made all three growl.

"You're on a nickname basis with the king?" Kayden asked.

"This is not the time for this!" I shouted and pulled my hand out of Mason's.

Kayden gave Trey the book, picked me up, and they started running again. "Where are we headed to, exactly?"

I clutched the necklace in one hand and said, "I'm hoping the necklace will give us a portal. One that we can take to get home." I knew the portals were the Grand Advisor's doing, but I had to keep playing dumb to some of his schemes.

"Princess!" Jol bellowed from somewhere behind us.

"Shit! He's faster than I thought he would be," I whined. Mason started to turn, but I shouted, "Just run!"

He growled, but they kept going.

"Please, necklace. Please give us an escape," I begged.

The sooner I could get them home and get the book to my family, the sooner I could come back and work things out with Jol. I hadn't lied. I would one hundred percent return to help them. Even if it meant possibly coming to face him and fight him.

A portal opened about fifty yards in front of us. "There!" I shouted and pointed.

The guys sprinted forward and we made it through the portal.

Pushing out of Kayden's arms, I turned to face the portal, fear coursed through me as I watched Jol run closer.

"You!" Jol snarled and pointed at Kayden.

My eyes widened and mouth opened. Kayden? It had been Kayden?

"I will have your head!" Jol bellowed.

"I'm sorry!" I shouted at him. "I can't let you kill them!"

The portal started to close and I backed up, arms out to make the guys back up as well. "I'm sorry, Jol."

His eyes bore into mine. "This isn't over, Little Queen."

I nodded. "I know."

The portal closed and I fell into Kayden. "We're in so much trouble," I whispered as tears streamed down my face.

AFTER BEING HUGGED and kissed by every single one of my family members and Maya, an emergency meeting was called with the full family so I could give them an update. I took the necklace, wrapped in a cloth again, and set it outside away from the house, just in case I was right that the Grand Advisor could hear us through it.

When my phone connected to the network, hundreds of missed calls and text messages came through, making my phone vibrate and beep so much it grew really hot. I ended up turning it off and leaving it in my room.

Standing before my family, I took a breath and tried to gather my thoughts.

"I wasn't there very long," I started, "but over the past two weeks—"

"Weeks?" Mom asked, interrupting me. "Lily, you were there *months*."

My mouth dropped. "Wh-What?"

Everyone nodded.

"Time must move differently from there to here," Nana Jolie said.

That explained the trio's beards.

Scrubbing a hand down my face, I said, "Okay, well, there's a lot you need to know and not much time to tell you."

It took three hours to explain everything about their world, their people, and the war, plus the plague that had happened to them. When I finished, they stared at me like I had grown a second head. I had left out the part about me being part demon. I felt like that should be shared with my parents first.

"I know it's a lot to take in," I whispered, "but they aren't our true enemies. Nana Jolie, Auntie Leona, I'm ninety percent certain the Grand Advisor is a siren in disguise or a hybrid siren and mage, and think the portals are his doing ... somehow. And I think he uses the necklace to listen to what the wearer is discussing."

"Well, fuck," Great Aunt Leona said and sighed, dropping her head back to look up at the ceiling.

"Do you think it could be another lost brother?" Nana Jolie asked Grandpa Nico.

"I can't rule it out as a possibility," he muttered and scowled deeply. It had come to light that Grandpa Nico's father, who had been King of the Mages then, had had several children outside of his marriage.

"I think we can help them," I said. "I was able to use

my limited elven powers to get one of their plants to grow, so if we had other, more powerful, elves go with me, they could help the rest of their land. We could take some of our crops, get them to grow there, and help them fix their world."

"Do they want help?" Trey asked. "If the Grand Advisor is right, they will only focus on fighting us."

"Jol ... their king, he wants his people to survive, and if we can give him an option that doesn't include bloodshed, I'm certain he will take it." Biting my lip, I admitted, "He is upset that his to-be mate was killed, but I'm certain that I can convince him to—"

"Wait, you're planning to go *back*?" Trey asked, scowling.

"Yes," I said and nodded. Why was that even a question?

Everyone blinked at me, shocked and upset.

"You've been gone for months," Mason whispered, "but you want to go back to face him? He was hunting us down in full armor and—"

"He wasn't hunting me," I clarified. "He was after Kayden."

"You think he won't harm you now that he knows that Kayden is the one who killed his to-be mate?" Great Grandpa Dan asked.

"He won't," I said, though, if I was being one hundred percent honest, there was at least a ten percent chance in my mind that he might turn on me. Though, as their long-lost demon princess, a royal from the bloodline he had sworn to protect, I hoped it was really more like a one percent chance. "I am going to bring vegetables back with me that are resilient, plant them in his garden, and nurture them to life to prove he doesn't need to come to our world. To show him there is another way."

"No," Mason growled. "You are not going back there."

"You don't make decisions for me," I snarled.

"It's out of the question," Caleb snapped. He had been quiet the entire time, so it shocked me when he spoke so sternly.

"Dad, I can talk to King Jolmach. I can convince him war isn't the only option. We have a bit of a friendship now and he will listen to me. You have to believe me." I understood they were worried about my safety, but this was something I had to do.

"You want to risk your life, face off against a demon warrior who could kill you just as easily as listen to you, to convince him to let us regrow crops for him?" Branson asked. He shook his head. "It's out of the question, Lily. Absolutely not."

"I am an adult and I am making this decision on my own," I said with a glare.

"You are an adult, but you are under my power," Caleb snarled. "You will do as you are ordered and I order you *not* to go back to that world and risk your life. We will send someone else who—"

"Who else?" I hissed, getting to my feet and slamming my hands on the table. My hair glowed bright, rainbows dancing around the room, drawing all of their gazes. "Who else has a rapport with them? Who else spent time getting to know them on a personal level? None of you! I can do this! I *will* do this!"

"Let's discuss this calmly and in more detail," Mom said coolly. "If we are going to send them crops, which crops?"

All of my adoptive fathers had their arms crossed over their chests, brows furrowed, and I knew our argument was far from over. Trey, Mason, and Kayden would be on their side as well, so I was going to have my work cut out for me convincing them to let me go back.

"Potatoes would be a good start," I said and sat again. "Plants that are hard to kill and grow in rough climates and provide good nourishment."

"We can send dried meats as well," Triston commented. "Things that don't spoil quickly."

"Yes," I said with a wide smile, "that's perfect. They do have refrigerators of a sort, though I'm not sure if it's all of them or just in the castle."

We discussed other options for over an hour before we decided to call it a night. Mom pulled my fathers away before they could restart our argument about me returning.

Heading to the couch, I plopped down and closed my eyes with a deep sigh. The longer I stayed here, the less time I had to convince Jol not to attack. In truth, I had no idea if he would launch the attack now, at any moment, or what steps they needed before attacking us.

"Nothing will be decided tonight," Trey whispered as he sat beside me. "You should get some rest."

Mason sat on my other side, picked up my hand, and rubbed his face on it. "We missed you so much, Lily."

Opening my eyes, I looked into his troubled ones. "I'm sorry it was so long for you all." Turning to look at Trey and then at Kayden, who was next to Trey, I said, "It really was only a few weeks for me."

Trey patted my hand. "We're just glad that you weren't hurt or imprisoned, or anything worse."

He meant tortured.

"I was treated very well," I assured them. "The bed I slept on was even softer than my own here."

"Are ..." Kayden paused in his question, but after a breath he continued. "Are you trying to go back because of the king?"

My brows furrowed as I contemplated his question, then realized what he was asking. "Oh, no, it's not like that with Jol and I. We're friends." Though, the Grand Advisor had said I was a good match for Jol. And the kiss Jol had given me had confused me. And we had eaten in his room and ... no, no, it wasn't like that. Jol was just happy I was helping them. "Jol is kind and treated me well, but there are no amorous feelings between us," I assured them.

Trey and Kayden seemed to relax a bit more at my assertion, but Mason still sat tensely beside me, his hand holding mine.

I set my hand on his cheek, making him look up into my eyes. "I'm here and I'm safe."

Pulling me onto his lap, he held me gently with his head rested against my shoulder. "It hurt so much to be apart from you."

Kayden came to sit on Mason's other side, so all three could touch me simultaneously.

"Thank you, for coming to rescue me," I whispered. "When I heard you were there ... it made my heart soar."

"We will always come for you," Trey said, and rested his forehead against my other shoulder.

"We would have come sooner if we could have," Kayden whispered, "but there were no portals."

Mason remained silent as he held me, seeming to still need to confirm I was actually here with him.

Exhaustion hit me and I yawned. "I'm sorry, all the talking and drama seems to have exhausted me."

They all stood to leave.

"We're going to stay at Ezio's tonight," Trey informed me. "We'll be back tomorrow morning, okay?"

I nodded. "Okay."

He leaned down, kissed my cheek, and said, "Sleep well, Lily."

Kayden kissed the side of my head before following Trey.

Mason lingered, his thumb stroking the back of my hand.

"Mas?" I asked softly.

"I've never been lucky in life," he whispered. "So, when you disappeared, I feared the worst. However, I've always felt a connection to you, one that thankfully stayed even after you removed the shadow power, and that connection didn't disappear when you did. So, I did everything I could to try to find a portal, a way to get back to you. I even defied your father, our alpha and king, in doing so."

My eyes widened. What did he mean by that?

"No matter what happens, know that I will always, *always* find a way to you." He looked deep into my eyes and said, "My life is with you, Lily, wherever you decide to go. So, please, if you leave, if you go back, take me with you."

Tears brimmed in my eyes and I wrapped my arms

CATHERINE BANKS

around his neck, and buried my nose against his throat, drawing in his familiar and comforting scent. "I didn't leave you on purpose, Mason. I did not teleport there of my own free will. And I didn't have a chance to return to you before you showed up. I swear. I would have returned at the earliest opportunity that I could."

His arms wrapped around me and he hugged me tight. "Swear you won't leave me behind?"

"I swear I won't purposefully leave you behind," I whispered. It was the best promise I could make, considering the portals opened whenever they damn well pleased.

"I don't want to leave you," he whispered. "I just got you back."

"Too bad, pup," Mom said. "You're not mated yet and she needs sleep. You can come back in the morning."

He huffed slightly and gripped me tighter.

"You were going to tell us something before you left," he whispered. "Will you tell us tomorrow?"

Right, I had forgotten about that.

I nodded and sat back to smile at him. "Yes."

He kissed me lightly on the lips, lingering a moment to inhale my breath, and reluctantly released me to leave the house.

Mom set her hand on my shoulder and said, "Go to bed, sweetheart. Tomorrow is going to be busy and chaotic."

I hugged her and rested my head on her chest. "I fear that the chaos is only beginning." Remembering the other information I had to share, my throat tightened as I said, "I need to speak to you, Tony, and all of my fathers before we go to bed."

She scowled, but nodded and went to gather them into the dining room.

As I stood before them, I felt a deep sense of worry. Although they had always treated me as their own, I wasn't their blood. Would they see me differently once they found out I had demon blood? Once they realized that I wasn't a hybrid like them, but a demon hybrid? Would my loving, wonderful family, my adoptive mother, my brother, and my four fathers, would they disown me and cast me aside?

I drew in a deep breath and said, "There's something else I didn't tell everyone. Something I wanted to tell you all first."

"Go on," Caleb urged, clearly worried, as he sat up straighter at the table.

It was best just to rip it off, like removing a bee stinger. Taking a deep breath and praying I wasn't about to be kicked out, I said, "I'm part demon. According to them, I am a royal who went missing when I was a child. I'm ... they claim I'm a long-lost Princess of the Demons."

They blinked at me silently, eyes wide as they absorbed what I had said.

"And ... there's a prophecy." I pulled out my book and turned to the page, handing it to Mom to read. I pulled out the snake and lily charm and set it on the center of the table. "I met with a group of females, who are the few who keep written records, and after seeing me shift, they all believe I am the prophesized one. Prophesized by my grandmother, the former queen. That's why I must go back. Jol isn't just a friend. The demons, they are my people, and I need to save them."

CHAPTER
TEN

Getting so many strong-willed, alpha male, growly kings to agree on anything was like herding cats.

When they were as stubborn as I was, that meant that we were at a stalemate. My hair had been glowing for hours now and I constantly oozed black smoke, though the snake stayed inside, thankfully.

"Ordering me or forbidding me from going won't stop me," I said sternly.

"You can't just admit to your king that you're going to defy him," Great Nana Kara said and tsked.

"When he's being unreasonable and won't listen to reason, he should know the order is stupid and shouldn't be given in the first place," I said and hissed.

"You don't need to go," Riddick said. "We can send someone else who is more powerful to—"

"More powerful? Why would you need someone more powerful? Unless ..." My eyes widened. "You're planning to attack him? You can't! He is not our enemy. How many times do I have to explain everything to you?"

"How many times do I have to tell you that you aren't going?" Caleb growled. His eyes were glowing, which meant he was pissed because he had really good control of his emotions ... most of the time.

I was pissed, too. Even after everything I had told them last night, he was still trying to forbid me from going back.

"We're getting nowhere arguing about this," I said sternly. "None of you can access the portals, which means you can't go there or come back."

"We can when you give us the necklace," Branson said.

My hand shot up to where the necklace normally was, but it was hidden outside. I hissed at them, "No! Giving you the necklace won't help you get there. Did you not listen to what I said about it?"

"Okay, everyone, let's take a deep breath," Great Aunt Leona said and used her powers to send a wave of calmness to all around the room.

The calmness reminded me of something Jol had said, that they had seen me before I came.

I said, "The Grand Advisor was using the necklace to spy on us. I feel a thousand times lighter when I'm not wearing it."

"I knew we should have forced her to remove it sooner, before she was teleported," Branson said, and growled.

"I know you all view me as the little girl that you adopted," I whispered as I looked at my adoptive parents. "But I'm not a scared little hybrid child. This is something that needs to be done. We have to help them. There are orphaned children starving there," I said softly. "They need help. I need to help them."

"Why does it have to be you?" Great Aunt Leona asked gently.

"Let me do this," I begged.

"Tell us why it's so important to you, Lily," Nana Jolie urged.

"Why do you need to help them?" Great Grandpa Dan asked.

Taking a breath, I knew the only way to convince them was to bare my soul and admit what I barely acknowledged myself. "What's the point of being a princess, of being adopted into this family of powerful royals, if I'm useless? What have I accomplished in this life so far? Besides ..." I might as well admit it to the rest of my family, though I worried what the trio would think. After a big breath, I blurted, "I'm not just a hybrid and princess of our world. I'm a hybrid and princess of both worlds. I'm the Demon Princess."

If a butterfly flapped its wings, it would have sounded like an explosion in the silence.

Grandpa Nico stood slowly with his eyes fixed on me. "Say that again."

"Nico," Nana Jolie warned.

"My grandmother was the Queen of Demons, the ruler before Jol. They call her Third to Reign. She had premonitions and could use the shadow powers like I can. My parents took me from the demon world and hid me here. I think ... I think to get me away from the Grand Advisor."

"You're a demon?" Great Grandpa Dan asked.

"Part, yes."

Mason walked around the table opposite Grandpa Nico, focused on him and his movements.

I was also focused on him, not sure why he was walking towards me.

"I found out while I was there. I felt a kinship to them, a draw, like I do hybrids, and thought perhaps they were part hybrid, but it is because I'm part demon. I'm sorry I didn't tell you all sooner, but I was worried what you might think and—"

Grandpa Nico stopped next to me, Mason on my other side, body tensed. Grandpa Nico looked down at me, a deep scowl on his face a moment before he smiled and hugged me, patting the back of my head. "My sweet Lily-poo. Were you really worried we would disown you or hate you? Such nonsense going through your head."

"Y-You don't?" I stammered, stunned.

"We don't care if you're a warthog," Great Grandpa Dan said. I looked over at him and he smiled. "You are our family and family doesn't care if you're a princess or a pauper. We love you and always will."

Tears sprang to my eyes and dripped down my cheeks before I could stop them.

Nana Jolie and Great Aunt Leona rushed out of their chairs and around the table to take me from Grandpa Nico and hug me.

"It's alright," Great Aunt Leona crooned, her powers easing some of my anxiety. "We love you, silly Lily. You could be a hellhound and we'd still love you."

"That hellhound friend of yours was pretty adorable," Nana Jolie said as she stroked a hand down my hair.

Once back in their seats, I said, "Now you understand. I am more than a hybrid of our world; I'm part demon and they are my people as well. I can do this. Let me do this. I *must* do this."

Dad stood so quickly that his chair flew backwards and shattered against the wall behind him. He turned and stomped out of the house.

Great Grandpa Dan stood slowly and said, "I'll go speak to him."

"I'll come, too," Grandpa Foxfire said and followed.

"You're ... part demon?" Trey asked.

I nodded, afraid to look at them.

"So that darkness, that smoky power wasn't from the spell that hit you?" Nana Jolie asked.

"No, it seems that spell just unlocked my demonic powers. Powers that come from their third monarch, the one who wrote the prophecy about me, my biological grandmother," I explained.

After filling them all in on the additional information, it was incredibly quiet.

Mason, Kayden, and Trey left the house together, making my chest ache.

"Let's get back to our list," Great Nana Kara said. "We decided on the first few plants to see if they can survive. My concern is water. Did they have a water source?"

"I didn't see any, but I didn't get to travel very far. They claim their water sources weren't ruined, but that they are underground and they have to haul it up." Turning to Great

Aunt Leona I asked, "Is it possible for a siren to cause a mass hallucination that lasts for years and effects those who newly enter the world?"

"A spell of that magnitude seems impossible," she whispered. "I can't see how they could do it to brand new people who haven't met them yet and have it spread all across the entire world. To be that powerful would be unheard of."

Mason, Trey, and Kayden returned, standing by the wall instead of sitting near me again. Was this their answer? Were they going to stop courting me now?

"What if the world really is burnt," Mason whispered.

"What do you mean?" I asked.

"Think about the more logical explanation for this," he said and started pacing across the room. "If he planted a false memory into their minds, of the war and plague, but then he burned everything to line up with that story, he wouldn't need to alter any newcomer's minds."

"Why not make himself king then?" I asked. "Wouldn't it be more likely that he'd use those powers to become the ruler?"

"Being a ruler isn't always fun. Being the advisor who tells the king what to do is a far better position," Nana Jolie said.

Shit, that did seem more logical.

Rubbing my temples, I asked, "So, he implanted false memories, including putting himself as Grand Advisor, destroyed the world, all for what end game?"

Grandpa Nico said, "To take over our world. Once the demons wreak havoc here and take over, he will be one of the most powerful beings with no one to tell him what to do.

Even if the demons get wiped out, he's still safe and can rule in that world or come here and assume a new identity."

"If he is this powerful, then he could take any form he wanted," Great Aunt Leona said and stared into my eyes. "He could assume the king's form to deceive you."

"How does the necklace play into it?" Mason asked.

"I've been thinking about that," Grandpa Nico said. "If he used the gem as a window of sorts, a looking stone, he could see what you're seeing, which means when you were looking for a portal, he could have opened that one in front of you when you were fleeing."

"Portals can only be opened to places you've been before," Mom said and looked at Grandpa Nico for confirmation. He nodded. "That means, the Grand Advisor has to be from our world."

"And had traveled all across it," Kayden said. "The portals have opened all over the world, not just in Jinla."

My eyes widened. "He was able to open the portal in our lands because he saw it through the necklace."

Branson, Triston, and Riddick growled at the realization.

"He is determined to start a war," I whispered. "So, what can I do to stop him?"

"We," Mason said. "What can *we* do to stop him?"

"If too many of us go, King Jolmach is going to assume it's to fight," Nana Jolie said. "It's better if we only send a couple people."

"I don't think you three should go," Mom said softly to Mason, Trey, and Kayden. "You've been the main ones killing their people and I doubt they're so quick to forgive."

As much as I didn't want to admit it, she was right.

"Kayden can't go back," I reminded them. "Jol wants revenge still."

"What if that didn't even happen?" Nana Jolie asked. "What if that is a planted memory, too?"

"I have to convince Jol he has a false memory in order for him to get rid of the false memories?" I asked.

Great Aunt Leona nodded. "It's not easy to remove planted memories. Most of the time it's only possible when the person with the false memories finds the crack in the spell that's wrapped around their mind and breaks it. At least that's how Jolie and I did it when it happened to us. Or using the spell I taught you to burn it all out. It can be done by someone else, if they are powerful enough, but most times it must be done by themselves."

There was a way, though, I just had to convince Jol to look at his mind and memories to see if they truly were planted.

"I need some air," I said and hurried out of the house. Heading to the barn, I shifted and slid into my pool, closing my eyes and holding my breath as I lay along the bottom of the shallow water.

This was all too much. I wasn't strong enough or had the right powers to fight a siren-mage hybrid. As much as I hated to admit it, I needed at least Dad to go with me.

When Jol felt his power, I was certain he would simply attack him and not listen to me.

If I talked to Jol first, before we involved the others, perhaps that could work. I would avoid the Grand Advisor, speak to Jol, and return. Wait, I couldn't return without the Grand Advisor opening a portal for me.

Mom was better at portals than Dad, but she didn't have powers as strong as Dad when it came to siren and mage abilities. The perks of him being a true hybrid.

They couldn't open a portal to the demon world because they'd never been there, but there might be a way with one of my powers.

Shifting into my human form, I sat on my heat rock and remembered all the times I'd watched Grandpa Nico training Mom and Dad on portals. I was part mage, so it was possible that I could do it.

Closing my eyes, I pictured the bedroom I'd used. Drawing on my powers, I started drawing a circle in the air, imagining it opening to the bedroom.

When I opened my eyes, I found no portal.

I did find a scowling Mason.

"Were you just trying to create a portal?" he asked and folded his arms across his chest.

"I was seeing if I could do it." I shrugged nonchalantly, like he hadn't just caught me. "Turns out I cannot."

"You were going to leave without me," he accused.

"No, I was seeing if I could create the portal," I countered.

"And what if it worked? Would you have called me for to come or would you have stepped through?"

I was not answering that.

"I think I have a plan," I said as I walked by him and toward the barn's door. "I've just got to convince our dear king to it."

Mason grabbed my arm, stopping me. "Do you swear you aren't interested in him?"

"Who?"

"You know who," Mason whispered.

Turning to face him, I set my hands on either side of his face and said, "I am not interested in King Jolmach in a romantic or sexual way."

"I know I will share you with my packmates, with Trey and Kayden, but I do not want to share you with others," Mason whispered.

Squishing his cheeks, I said, "Silly, birdie, I don't want others." Spinning on my heel, I skipped out of the barn, looked over my shoulder and said, "Come on, I've got to tell them my plan."

When we returned to the house, I was glad to see everyone present.

"I have an idea," I said to get everyone's attention.

"Besides creating portals on your own?" Mason taunted.

Mom and Dad's eyes widened.

"You didn't?" Mom gasped.

"I can't create portals," I said and waved my hand dismissively. "Listen. Here's the plan. Mom and Dad are going to go with me to the demon world, straight to the castle to speak to Jol ... King Jolmach. We're going to explain everything to him. Then, we're going to come back, get the necklace, and go back to him, pretending it's our first time talking to him and Jol is going to threaten us and fight Mom and Dad, convincing the Grand Advisor, who will be watching through the necklace, that the war is still on. Jol will continue to play along with the farce, but when we face off on the day of the war, we will instead work together to defeat the Grand Advisor. Once he is out of the way, then we can help with their world's regrowth."

"Why Caleb and Ember?" Grandpa Nico asked.

"Mom can create portals to take us to and from their world. Dad can fight the best and is the most resistant to siren abilities. And I will play the pathetic little princess bringing not just her king and queen, but her mommy and daddy to talk to Jol to try to keep the peace."

"I'm going," Mason snapped. "You promised."

"You'll have to stay in bird form," I said.

He nodded. "Fine."

"There are so many ways this could go wrong," Riddick said. "I don't like you three going without more backup."

"More backup will look like an invasion," I countered.

"How are you going to get there first?" Grandpa Nico asked. "Neither of them has been there to be able to create a portal."

"I've been there and I can share that memory with Mom."

"Wait, what?" Great Aunt Leona asked.

"Yeah, what?" Mom asked.

Looking down at the table I said, "That's one of my other new powers."

"Speak up, brat, we can't hear you," Great Nana Kara said.

"It's one of my other powers," I said louder and raised my head. "I can share memories directly to another person's mind."

"How many other powers are there that you haven't told us about?" Dad asked and folded his arms over his chest.

111

"I don't know, a few."

"Ticks on a tortoise, Lily. Why haven't you told us about this before now?" Mom asked.

"There are some things that happened while I was at college that I don't want to relive, okay?"

"No, it's not okay," Kayden said and narrowed his eyes at me. "You're supposed to tell us—"

"I handled it on my own and everything's fine. Look, I got the shadow power under control, too." Summoning the power, the smoky snake swirled around my arm and transformed into a cobra shape, hood flared as it showed off. Sending it back, I said, "Back to the topic at hand. What do you think?"

"I think you should tell us what other powers you have," Trey muttered.

"I think it's a good option," Dad said, "but if I were to have a powerful alpha show up unannounced at my house, I definitely wouldn't be up for tea and cookies."

"That's why you're going as a wolf while hiding your alpha presence and Mom's going as a rabbit until I can explain enough to him that he won't freak out."

"It sounds simple, but there are so many things that could go wrong," Nana Jolie whispered.

"That's why we'll have a backup plan," Dad said. "Especially considering the timeframe difference for their world and ours."

"And what does this backup plan entail?" Mom asked.

"Well, it starts with the necklace," he began.

CHAPTER
ELEVEN

Kayden pulled me out of the meeting, out of the house, and to the barn.

"What's up, Kay?" I asked, confused why he pulled me out without a word and so far away. There were still several things to finalize before we left.

Kayden spun, gripped the back of my neck, and kissed me, his tongue sweeping in and stroking mine.

My hands went around his back, clutching his shirt.

We had never kissed like this, so passionately, so full of need.

He pulled back and rested his forehead against mine. "I don't want you to go," he whispered. "I don't want to be separated from you again."

I rubbed his back as we stood together. "I'm sorry." There was nothing else I could say. I wasn't going to back down on going.

"It's killing me to know you might be gone for a month or more again," he choked. "I just got you back."

"I can't promise you how long I'll be gone, but I can promise you that I will do everything in my power to return as soon as possible. I'll stay with my parents and I—"

"Why are you taking Mason?" he asked softly, his words laced with jealousy.

"Jol will kill you if he sees you again. Trey doesn't have a smaller form, and I figured you would be happy as long as at least one of you three went with me."

Taking his hand, I tugged him towards the door. "I need to get Trey and Mason so I can talk to you three."

His eyes widened and he followed me silently.

After grabbing Mason and Trey from the room where everyone was still discussing the plans and alternate plans, we went up to my room. Shutting the door behind me, I realized my room was rather small with three, adult, alpha males inside.

Kayden sat on my bed, playing with the pillow he'd given me.

Mason sat in my desk chair, spinning slowly.

Trey stood by my closet, looking at the picture of us and Maya playing in the lake on clan grounds. Even though he was a dragon prince, he spent a lot of his life here with us.

"What I was going to tell you before I was teleported has changed," I admitted softly.

All three turned to face me, scowling.

"What does that mean?" Trey asked.

"Originally, I was going to say that I wanted to court you three exclusively," I explained.

Their eyes widened and Mason got to his feet.

"However, I don't want that anymore."

Kayden's hand clenched my pillow and he asked, "Because of Jol?"

Being around Jol, seeing his world and the destruction was a reason, but not for the reason he meant.

The three of them practically vibrated with jealousy and barely contained rage. I needed to be blunt instead of beating around the bush so they didn't take it wrong or misunderstand.

"What I want is for you three to become my mates," I said. "If you'll have me."

"Yes," Mason said immediately.

"Wait," Trey said, causing Mason to growl. "Why the change?"

"Who cares?" Kayden said and stood. "My answer is yes."

Turning to face Trey fully, I explained, "Seeing their world, the devastation, and hearing his story of losing the female he had wanted, it hurt. My soul hurt to realize how spoiled, how utterly out of touch I am. I have three handsome, strong, and wonderful men who were my best friends, who are always trying to protect me, even when I can't see it. My fears, my self-consciousness, it is all so small, so insignificant, and all it has done is cause drama and issues. Although I tried to hide it, I tried to run from it, and dismiss it. I love you three. You've had my heart since we were teenagers, probably earlier, though I didn't realize it then. I don't know what the future will hold, I don't know if my plan will work or if we will face a war unlike anything we've faced before. However, I do know that not admitting my feelings, not admitting that there is not and will never be another group or individual outside of you three for me, is only hurting you."

Trey walked to me, cupped my cheek, and said, "I'm glad you can finally admit it."

I opened my mouth, but he cut me off with a kiss that made my toes curl. How were they so good at kissing? Not that I was complaining.

"Are you three sure? I did just tell you that I'm part demon, remember?"

"We don't care what your bloodlines are," Trey said. "All we care about is that you are ours."

"Lily!" Mom called.

"I know it's bad timing," I said, "but when I get back, we will get bloodstones and complete our mating bonds, okay? After the meeting, tonight, will you mark me?"

Trey smirked, "I've been waiting almost twenty years to hear you say those words." He rubbed his thumb across my cheek, kissed it, and opened my door. "We better hurry. I don't want to face an angry Caleb."

"Yeah, you already made him break a chair today," Kayden said as he pushed my lower back, forcing me out of the room.

Everyone looked at us with varying faces.

"What?" I asked Nana Jolie.

She shrugged and half-smiled. "Nothing."

"Why'd you call me?" I asked. "Did you decide something?"

"Can you share the memory with me?" Mom asked.

My eyes narrowed in suspicion. "Right now?" Looking

around, I realized Caleb and Grandpa Nico were missing. "Where's Dad?" Maya and Tony were missing, too.

"Nico is training him on a new spell," Nana Jolie said and immediately looked down at her hands in her lap.

Something was up. They were hiding something from me.

"We want to make sure you can do it and I can use what you show me to create the portal," Mom explained. "If we can't do it, then this entire discussion is wasted time."

That did make sense, but ...

"Okay," I agreed, walked to Mom, and placed my pointer finger on each of her temples. Closing my eyes, I brought up the memory in my mind of the bedroom I had stayed in at Jol's castle. I pictured everything as vividly as I could recall, including the smells.

She gasped and stepped back, eyes wide. "That's amazing, Lily."

"It's just a memory share," I said and shrugged nonchalantly. "In most circumstances, this won't help anyone."

Mom set her hand on my shoulder, frowned, and said, "Don't discount your powers, Lily. If this does work, this will be a huge magical improvement." Stepping back, she held out her finger, and opened a portal on the living room wall beside us. It opened and displayed the room, but the room was trashed, the bedding torn to shreds, and furniture destroyed.

My hands went to my mouth and tears filled my eyes. Had Jol done this because he thought I'd lied and abandoned him?

I approached the portal, but before I could step through, Mom closed it.

Mouth open to protest, I turned to say something, but Dad and Grandpa Nico stepped forward and whispered something beneath their breath. Black chains shot up out of the ground and wrapped around me.

"Dad!" I screamed in shock and struggled against the chains.

"I'm sorry, Lily, but I cannot let you go back. I cannot risk you," Dad whispered.

"Don't do this!" I shouted. "Don't do this to me!" Looking at Mason, Trey, and Kayden, I begged, "Please! Please!"

They stared at us all with wide eyes.

Mason and Kayden took a step forward, but Trey grabbed each of their shoulders. "I'm sorry, Lily, but we cannot defy your king's order."

Mom grabbed a bag from beside the table and hefted it over her shoulder. "When you're a parent, you'll understand."

"Mom, please. He doesn't know you! He's going to fight you! Let me go with you. He'll listen to me. I know he will."

"No, you *think* he will," Dad said and shook his head. He rested his hand on my cheek and said, "I know it hurts, but we are doing this to protect you."

Tears streamed down my face. "You're doing this to appease your need to protect me, your alpha instincts. If you'd use your humanity, you'd let me go."

"I almost lost you twice, I'm not going to let it happen a third time," he said and followed Mom.

"Grandpa, please let me go. Please! Why won't you listen to reason?" I screamed.

"We'll let him know you're being held by us against your will," Mom said, tears in her eyes.

"What happens when they don't come back?" I asked.

"Then I'll go," Grandpa Nico said. He tilted his head towards the open portal. "I've now seen the place so I can teleport."

They could go without me now. I was once again useless.

"I'm not going to stop," I said and bared my teeth at him. "I'm going to find my own way there. None of you can stop me." I looked at each of my family members and the trio, meeting all of their eyes. "All you've done is ensure I never trust you again."

Grandpa Nico sighed. "I figured you'd say something like that." He pressed his fingers to my head and my eyelids grew heavy. "I'm sorry, my granddaughter, but we protect our family."

"I'm not your family," I bit out just before the sleep spell fully took hold.

My entire body ached as I woke. Sitting up, I pressed a hand to my head. What day was it? How long had I been asleep?

"Lily," Mason whispered.

Turning, I realized that I was locked in one of the cells in our basement. Not only had they prevented me from going and knocked me out, they'd locked me in a magical prison.

Mason crouched outside of the cell door, his body curled in on itself.

"What do you want?" I hissed and turned back around to face the wall.

He whined. "We didn't know," he said urgently. "We were with you when they came up with the plan to keep you here. I swear, I swear on my shifter form that I didn't know."

I believed him, but I still didn't turn around.

"I'm going to get you out," he whispered.

"How long have I been asleep?"

"Four days."

Sucking in a sharp breath, my chest hurt at the betrayal.

"My parents?"

"We haven't heard from them."

Fuck.

Getting back to my feet, I approached the cell door. "How are you going to get me out? I thought only my parents could open these cells."

"I helped your dad one time and he gave me the ability to open them. It wasn't revoked because we both forgot about it."

"If you do this, he's going to punish you." While I wanted to be free, to help my parents, I needed him to be sure about helping me.

"A punishment from my king is better than you thinking that I could ever betray you like this."

"Does Trey know you're here?" I asked, scowling as I recalled him stopping Kayden and Mason.

"He knows I left, but since he's not a hybrid, I thought best to keep him in the dark as to my plans so the others couldn't get it from him and he won't be in trouble of helping you when he's not a hybrid."

"I need stuff to take to Jol," I said.

"We don't have time to go back to the house. Riddick, Branson, and Triston are there, growling and pacing. I grabbed the necklace, though." He held up the towel-wrapped necklace. "Since we can't make portals."

While I still suspected that the Grand Advisor was listening to us, it was necessary to find a portal.

"Okay, let me out," I said.

Mason reached forward, pressing his fingers against the lock, and whispered something beneath his breath. The cell unlocked and the door swung open.

Stepping out, I threw my arms around his neck and kissed him. "Thank you."

"Let's go," he said urgently and set the necklace in my hand.

I put it on and it sent a deep vibration throughout my body. There, at the edge of my mental barriers, I felt the siren magic intruding.

So, he was definitely a siren, then.

Mason slung a bag over his shoulder. "I have a few plants in here, and some snacks for us, but this was all I could bring."

I nodded. "It's fine." Gripping the necklace, I whispered, "Please, please let a portal appear." Admitting I knew it was him would give us away, so I needed to be sure to keep up the act.

Mason pushed open the external door of the basement at

the top of the stairs that led into the barn. Poking his head out, he looked and said, "Clear."

We hurried up into the barn, closing the door behind us, and a portal opened next to me.

I gripped Mason's hand, and we stepped through the portal.

"Lily!" Branson roared from the basement.

"Well, that was good timing," I whispered as I watched the portal close behind us.

Looking around, it took me a minute to get my bearings. We were in a village that looked like Talrinir's village.

"I don't know where we are," I said with a scowl.

"Uh, look behind you," Mason whispered.

I turned and my eyes widened at the female demons all brandishing weapons.

"Don't move," the one nearest us growled.

TWELVE

"We mean you no harm," I said and raised my hands to show her they were empty. "I'm here to help. I'm one of you, remember? King Jolmach is protecting me and I'm part demon."

She growled louder.

"Oh, Princess Thief!" Azgon shouted as she stepped out from the back of the group.

"Princess Azgon," I greeted.

"Princess?" the demon in front of us asked.

Azgon tittered. "You were gone so long. We thought you dead."

"So long?" I asked. "How long do you think I was gone?"

"Weeks," she said. "It's three weeks since Azgon saw you in the garden."

Why did time not move consistently?

"I need to speak with Jo ... King Jolmach."

"Oh, he's at the castle. Um, you should hurry. The rabbit

lady is in trouble, going to be killed I think." She pointed in the direction of the castle.

Gasping, I spun and started running. Mom. Mom had to be the rabbit lady she mentioned.

Mason kept pace with me, silent as he let me lead the way.

"You should shift into your raven form," I said as we neared the castle. "I don't want him to know you're a shifter yet if we can help it."

He huffed out a breath, but gave me the bag, shifted, and landed on my shoulder.

In front of the castle, at the edge where the city and castle grounds met, a platform had been built and atop it stood Jol and Mom. Mom was tied up with a blindfold on and a gag in her mouth.

Jol stood beside her, his spiked mace in his hand, a dark aura swirling around him.

"Wait!" I screamed as I charged forward.

Jol's head whipped up, eyes narrowed on me as I approached.

"Little Queen," he spat, fury etched across his face.

"Wait," I panted. "Please, listen to me."

"You sent them," he accused. "You sent powerful magic users to my castle!"

I shook my head. "I was coming back, I was working with them to get food and crops to bring you and your people."

"You've been gone weeks!" he bellowed.

Mom started struggling against her bindings and yelling, but her words weren't discernible. She was likely telling me to run, to flee, but I wouldn't. Not when she was in trouble.

There must have been a spell on her as well to prevent her from communicating mentally with me.

It worried me even more that Dad was nowhere to be seen.

Hopping up onto the platform, I held out my hand placatingly to Jol. "Time moves differently between our realms," I explained. "I swear, I was only gone a few days in my world and I spent those days arguing with my overprotective family. They locked me up and prevented me from coming back here."

Jol's fury turned into confusion. "Locked you up?"

I nodded. "They put me in a magical prison that I couldn't escape from. They were worried that you would hurt me if I came back. I tried to tell them that you wouldn't, that you would let me explain, but they didn't want to risk it. Please, please let me explain everything to you." Opening the bag, I pulled out a small pot with a sprout in it. "I've brought plants to try. I swear, Jol. I swear to you on my soul that I was coming back and would have been back sooner if I could have. Please, give me five minutes."

He growled and said, "Follow me." Turning to Zoman, who stood to his side, he ordered, "Take the woman to her cell."

Zoman nodded and grabbed Mom by the arm.

Remembering the necklace was around my neck, I unclasped it, which was much easier this time, and held the chain out to Mason. "Fly this away," I ordered him.

"No," he croaked.

Sighing, I stopped at the doorway to the castle. "Jol, one second," I called.

He turned to watch me.

Taking the necklace, I set it on the ground just outside the door, turned, and walked inside.

He opened his mouth, but I held my finger up to my lips and waved him forward.

His scowl deepened, but he turned and led me to his room.

Once inside with the door shut, Jol jerked me forward. The sudden jerk caused Mason to fall off my shoulder with a startled caw.

Jol pulled me into his chest and hugged me tightly. "You foolish female. Are you injured?"

I hugged him back despite my shock and shook my head. "I'm uninjured."

Pushing me back, he looked down into my face and said, "I thought you had abandoned me."

Smiling, I said, "You silly demon king, I never abandon my friends or my people, and you are both."

"You shouldn't have come," he whispered. "We've been working out a plan to get the Grand Advisor to show his true colors. You were safe at home, even if I didn't want you to be away." He paused and rested his hand against my cheek. "I am happy to see you."

"Was it you who thrashed my room?"

He smiled and shook his head. "That was Dhun."

My eyes widened. "Dhun?" Looking around I asked, "Where is he?"

"With your king," he said.

Mason shifted, pulled me back, out of Jol's arms, and

wrapped his arms around my upper chest. "Mine," he growled and bared his teeth.

Jol froze and looked down at me. "Who is this?"

"This is Mason, my to-be mate, one of them," I explained. "I promised him he could come this time. Please, don't hurt him. He isn't your enemy."

Jol relaxed a bit. "You better keep her safe."

Mason scoffed. "Have you met her? Do you know how difficult that is when she runs into the arms of demon kings?"

Jol laughed and Mason relaxed against me, but kept his arm around my chest.

"The necklace," I explained, "we think the Grand Advisor is using it as a mirror of sorts, a way to listen and or watch me. That's why I left it outside."

"Oh, that's what your parents meant," he said and nodded.

"It's possible there are other items, but I can't sense them or tell you what to look for."

"I will try to search on my own, thank you for the knowledge," he said.

"Where is my dad?" I asked.

"He and Dhun are exploring the world, trying to find other water sources and anything to expose the lies the Grand Advisor has been feeding us," he explained. "Don't worry about your mom, she's not in a real cell, but we've got to keep up appearances for the ruse we're playing. I had her on the platform to rally my people a bit, to keep them and the Grand Advisor thinking we're still going to have the battle."

"Should I go back?" I asked. "Back to my world?"

He reached out and took my hand. "I would prefer you to stay."

Mason growled again and the deep rumble vibrated against my back, making me smirk.

"How can I help with the ruse?" I asked.

"He'll need to pretend to be a true bird," Jol said and tilted his chin at my shoulder at Mason. "You'll have to become my prisoner."

Mason growled again.

Turning to look at him over my shoulder, I said, "You sure have been growling a lot lately."

"Says the woman doing things to make him growl." Jol laughed and released my hand. With a sigh he said, "It would be better for you to return to your world, even if I would rather you be here."

"I'm worried about the time differences," I said. "I think it has something to do with the Grand Advisor's memory altering."

"That could be," Jol said with a nod.

"How will we know when to come back if we leave?" I whispered. "What if we stayed hidden, in our animal forms, instead?"

He shook his head. "We believe he is able to use something to enhance his abilities and anyone who is here is affected, whether he speaks to them or not."

Sighing, I ran a hand down my face. "Of course it's not that simple."

"Doesn't that mean he knows we're here now?" Mason asked. "Should we leave before he comes here?"

"Let me show you what we brought," I said and set the bag on the coffee table and opened it fully.

Mason helped me pull the items out and set them on his dresser next to the items his people had given him.

My eyes widened when I saw the candy bar inside.

Mason muttered, "It used to be your favorite candy bar."

Kissing his cheek I said, "It still is." Taking it, I held it out to Jol, and showed him how to open it. "This is a type of dessert, it's called a candy bar."

Jol's eyes widened and he took it, popping the entire thing in his mouth. His eyes grew the widest I had ever seen them as he chewed it and swallowed. "That's delicious!" he exclaimed.

"When we come to our peace agreement, and you come visit my world, I'll take you to try all the best desserts and foods we have."

"You are a good friend," he said with a nod. His eyes narrowed and he said, "Unlike the Grand Advisor, who I had thought was my friend."

"Are you sure you want us to leave?"

He nodded. "I want you to be safe and you are safest in your world." Reaching over, he grabbed a communication stone. "I'm not sure if this will work in your world, but I will try to contact you with it if something happens. And you can use it to check in with me, since we aren't sure about the time differences."

I put it in my pocket and hugged him. "Please keep my family and yourself safe."

He hugged me back and said, "I will do my best. And I'll let your mom know you're safe."

I stepped back and smiled at him. "Thank you."

"To keep with our plan, you'll need to flee from the castle and I'll have to run after you like I'm hunting you," he said. His brows furrowed a moment. "Let's hope a portal appears for you to escape through."

It was possible he wouldn't create a portal, but I had a feeling he would. The less outsiders here, the more likely Jol would follow through on his plan.

"Oh, I almost forgot," Jol said and pulled a folded piece of paper from his pocket. "Your mom thought you might find a way here, or one of your friends, so she wrote something for you. I didn't read it, so not sure what it contains."

"Thanks," I said and put it in my pocket. Turning to Mason, I tapped my shoulder. "Time to go."

He sighed, shifted, and landed on my shoulder, nipping my hair in his beak.

We headed out of Jol's room and out the front door. I grabbed the necklace, put it on, and started running, imagining Jol after me and wanting to kill me.

Jol roared in the castle, the sound startled me and made me gasp. I increased my speed as true terror filled me for a moment.

"I will find you, Little Queen!" he bellowed.

Gripping the necklace, I whispered, "Please give me a portal. Please. I can't let him catch me!" The terror in my voice was only slightly faked since I could imagine what he would do, had we truly been enemies.

As I ran, I saw the Grand Advisor and a few other demons heading towards the palace. His eyes widened at the sight of me.

"I just want to go home!" I screamed and altered my trajectory so I wouldn't go near him.

Mason turned on my shoulder to face behind me.

A few seconds later, a portal opened in front of me, opening directly in front of my house.

I ran through and turned, watching as it started to close.

The Grand Advisor lowered his hand and gave me a bone-chilling smile and a little wave of his fingers before the portal closed. An awful feeling slithered down my spine, almost like a premonition in and of itself. Something awful was going to happen. He was going to do something truly despicable, but there was nothing I could do.

Taking the necklace off, I wrapped it in the towel again and put it back in the spot outside that I'd stored it last time.

Mason shifted, but stayed silent as we headed into the house.

Riddick, Branson, Triston, Grandpa Nico, Trey, and Kayden spun from their seats in the living room to look at us as we entered.

"I've confirmed the Grand Advisor is creating the portals," I said and headed towards the stairs. "Mason can fill you in more. I need a shower."

"Did you see your parents?" Grandpa Nico asked.

"Yes, they're working with Jol. Jol told me to come home to avoid getting entangled in the plan and any potential fight with the Grand Advisor."

"He didn't want you to leave at first," Mason mumbled.

I waved my hand. "Fill them in, please."

"Lily," Grandpa Nico called.

Turning, I said, "I'm not ready to talk to you yet." Looking at each of my fathers and Trey, I said, "Any of you."

The shower felt amazing and as I leaned my forehead against the cold tile, I thought over everything that had happened the past two weeks. So much had happened. So much had changed in such a short time.

Cleaned and refreshed, I dressed and grabbed the communication stone. Holding it tightly in my hand, I pictured Jol's face and asked, "Can you hear me?"

"Little Queen," Jol responded.

Sighing in relief, I flopped backwards onto my bed, still holding the stone. "At least this works."

"You made it safe?"

"Yes. I saw the Grand Advisor heading to you."

"Yes, he was trying to convince me to kill your queen, but I convinced him we need her for the battle."

"Please make sure you contact me if anything happens or you need me, okay?" Knowing they were there, and it was difficult for me to get there on my own worried me. If the Grand Advisor figured out that Jol had learned his secret, he could try to brainwash him again.

"I will do my best to be safe," he promised. "I have to go speak to my council."

"Bye, Jol."

"Bye, Little Queen."

I let the stone fall out of my hand, but then realized I could use it to communicate with Mom and Dad.

Picking it back up, I pictured Mom. "Mom, it's Lily. I just want you to know I'm back home and safe."

"Lily? How are you talking to me telepathically?"

"A communication stone Jol gave me."

"I'm sorry we locked you up. It wasn't my idea. I was very much against it."

"Time doesn't move consistently," I said, ignoring the statement. "I'm going to reach out to you guys every now and then to check in."

"Check in with your father. He and the pup are running around."

"Okay."

"I love you, Lily."

"Love you, too, Mama."

Picturing Caleb next, I whispered, "Dad? Can you hear me?"

"Lily?"

"I'm using a communication stone. I escaped and went to Jol, but he filled me in on your plan and I'm back home now."

"Of course you escaped and came here," he said.

"Have you found anything?"

"Yes, there is an entire section of their world that isn't destroyed. It's a beautiful oasis with thriving plant and animal life. The Grand Advisor put wards around it, so I didn't go in, and that's likely why their people don't know about it, but it exists."

"I knew there had to be something," I whispered.

"Tell my mom and Aunt Leona that we need them to defeat this guy. He's one hundred percent a hybrid of siren and mage. The scale with which he can use spells is astronomical. I don't think your mother and I can defeat him alone. I think he's using mana stones with stored magical energy to help boost his powers and spread the hallucination across the world."

I gasped. "That makes sense! There are mana stones all over the city and in the castle. "What's the plan?"

"We're going to continue with the war plan, have Jol bring your mother and I as captives, and when we're about to face off, everyone will turn on the Grand Advisor instead."

"How are you going to get him to go to the battle? He stays in his tower, away from everyone."

"Jol's working on that plan now. Don't worry."

"What do you want me to do here?"

"I will try to let you know the day the battle will happen. We'll need to evacuate Jinla, have all our strongest fighters gather in the main park, and prepare just in case things don't go the way we plan. I don't want to kill these people, but I won't let our people be massacred either."

"Okay."

"Stay safe, cub."

"You, too, Dad."

I sent a text to Maya to let her know I was out of the prison, safe, and would fill her in more tomorrow. She sent back a heart emoji, so I knew she wasn't mad at least. I needed to find time to reconnect with her.

Someone knocked on my door and I sighed softly. I should have known one of them would come up eventually.

"Who is it?" I asked.

"Me," Trey said.

"I'm not ready to talk to you."

"Too bad," he said and pushed open my door.

CHAPTER
THIRTEEN

Trey walked into my room and closed the door behind him. His eyes roved over me and he swallowed hard. "I know you're mad –"

"Not mad, hurt," I clarified.

He nodded and took a step closer to me. "I understand. I would feel the same way if the tables were turned. But, Lily, I couldn't disobey them. Even if I had stepped forward, they would have just held me back or thrown me into a cell as well."

"So, even if you were my mate, if they tell you to lock me up, you're going to?"

He growled deep in his chest and his eyes flashed, shifting into his dragon's eyes.

"It's been a long day," I said and pulled my blankets up over me. "Can you turn the light off on your way out?"

"I'm sorry," he said and knelt by the side of my bed next to me. "I'm sorry, Lily. Please, please understand."

Understanding why he did it wasn't the issue. I did understand. But I also felt betrayed.

"I let Mason go, knowing he was going to free you, knowing he would help you. I helped as much as I could."

"I know."

He grabbed my shoulder and rolled me onto my back so he could look at me. "Lily ..." His eyes widened when he saw the tears on my cheeks and he reached out, wiping them with his thumb.

"We're supposed to always have each other's backs," I reminded him. "We promised."

Throwing my covers back, he slid his arms beneath my back and legs, picked me up, sat on my bed, and set me on his lap. Wrapping his arms around me, cuddling me against his chest, he kissed my cheek and licked my tears. "I'm sorry. I swear, I won't ever let it happen again. I swear that you are the most important person in the world to me. All I want is for you to be safe and happy."

"That's not always a possibility for royalty, you know that."

He stroked a hand up and down my arm as he held me.

His warmth, his familiar scent, his body wrapped around mine, and his apology mixed together and leeched away all the pain and anger, leaving behind a deep exhaustion.

"We were so worried when you left," he whispered and tightened his arms around me. "We had no way of knowing if you were safe or not."

"How long were we gone for?"

"A few hours," he said.

Our timeframe matching had to be because the Grand Advisor hadn't been able to manipulate my mind.

Trey leaned back, cupped my cheek, and turned my head to face him. "Liliana, talk to me. You're keeping so much inside your head while your face is showing a variety of emotions. Talk to me."

"Stay with me tonight," I said and looked into his eyes. "Please."

His eyes widened a bit. "You want me to stay here?"

I nodded. "I have an awful feeling, one that's followed me since I was in the demon world. I ... I think something awful is about to happen."

Trey kissed my cheek and rested his forehead against the side of my head. "I won't let anything happen to you."

"Will you stay?"

He nodded. "Whatever you want."

Scooting over, he let me crawl out of his lap and lay down. Immediately, he spooned his body around mine and wrapped his arms around me, pulling me tight against him.

"Remember when we used to camp out?" he asked. "How mad Caleb was at first and how Ember convinced him to let us stay?"

There were many nights that Trey, Mason, Kayden, Tony, Maya, and I spent simply living in the forest, sitting together around a fire, then cuddling together to sleep. We'd done it during the summer and fall months from the time I was six until we were twelve. Dad had been nervous about boys and girls being alone together, but Mom reminded him that we were gallivanting around our territory all the time alone and we hadn't gotten into trouble yet. He finally caved.

"Those were some of the best nights of my life," Trey whispered and kissed the back of my head. "Being with you for as long as I wanted. Just existing. No royal training, politics, or enemies. Just us being us."

"Then we had to grow up and the fun ended," I whispered.

He nuzzled my neck and kissed it softly. "Whenever we had a particularly bad battle or my mom would hound me about getting a mate, it was those memories that helped me get through it. You've always been the light to escape my darkness. I'm sorry about the years apart. I'm sorry you had to face things on your own and you thought we didn't care for you. I will spend the rest of my life ensuring you know how much I love you. Ensuring I do everything in my power to make you happy."

"Trey?"

"Yeah?"

"Mark me?"

His body shuddered behind me. "You're sure?"

I rolled over to face him and nodded. "I am."

Brushing my hair back from my face, he said, "Answer something first?"

"What?"

"Are you sure there's nothing between you and the demon king? Mason told us how he treated you."

Smiling, I tapped the tip of his nose and asked, "Are you jealous, Prince Trey?"

"That's what I need to know, if I should be jealous."

"No, I am not interested in the demon king. Like I told you, my heart belongs to you three and has forever."

"And forever after?" he asked, his lips so close to mine that our breaths mingled.

"Through this lifetime and any future ones."

His lips pressed gently against mine as his hand slid around my side, to my back, and pulled me flush against him. His erection pressed into me and I whimpered.

He licked the seam of my lips and I opened them, letting him deepen the kiss. He kissed me slow and thoroughly. Leaning up, he pushed me onto my back, kissed his way from my lips, down my jaw, and to my neck. Reaching down, he slid his hand beneath my pajama pants waistband, his fingers sliding through my slick folds.

His breath hitched. "So wet for me, hm?"

"Always," I responded truthfully.

"I'm going to make you come, and then when you're about to come the second time, I'm going to mark you."

"Yes," I breathed.

He thrust his fingers inside of me and we both moaned.

"You have to be quiet," he reminded me. "The others are downstairs and we don't want them coming to investigate before we finish."

I nodded and gripped his muscular arms, reveling in the way his triceps flexed as he moved.

Dipping his head back down, he nipped at my neck, my collarbone, and my shoulder. "Where do you want my mark, Lily? On your neck? Your shoulder?"

"Somewhere visible," I answered.

He groaned and thrust his fingers into me faster. "Good answer, Princess."

I gripped his shoulders, my eyes closing as I felt my orgasm already building.

"After I mark you, I'm going to fuck you until your legs are jelly. Until you're covered in my scent and there is no mistake that you're mine."

"Yes," I whispered, my breaths coming in fast pants the closer to my orgasm I grew.

He adjusted the angle of his fingers and within seconds of stroking me, I came, having to bite his shoulder to keep from screaming out. "That's my girl," he purred and resumed kissing and licking my neck. "One more time and I'll mark you."

"Please," I begged as he increased his pace.

"Mm, don't beg, Princess. Tell me what you want. Order me."

"Harder," I said and squirmed to try to adjust the angle.

He shuddered and bit my neck gently. "Yes."

As he obeyed, my orgasm crested, and I whispered, "I'm close."

"Orders?"

"Mark me."

"What was that?" he teased and started to slow down.

"Faster and mark me, now," I ordered and hissed softly.

His fingers moved faster and as my orgasm hit me, he bit down on my neck, making the orgasm even stronger.

My mouth opened to cry out and I had to cover my mouth with my hand to stop the scream as stars danced across my vision from the pure euphoria.

Panting, I felt like my heart might burst through my chest with how hard it beat.

He licked the mark and said, "I've been dreaming of this night, pleasuring myself to the thought of doing this, for a decade."

"What?" I gasped.

Lifting his head, he smiled and said, "You've always been the one for me. I was just too scared to admit to you how much you owned me. That you own my soul."

Looking into his piercing green eyes, I said, "You're not done yet, Prince Trey."

He arched a brow.

"Didn't you say you were going to cover me in your scent?" Pulling my shirt off and shimmying out of my pajama pants, I lay, fully naked, in front of him. "I've yet to be covered in your scent."

He stood out of the bed, stripped out of his clothes, and my mouth watered at the sight of his erection. He was average length, but thick.

"Like what you see, Princess?" he asked, a cocky smirk on his face.

I nodded and crooked my finger at him. "Get over here and put that inside of me."

"Who am I to deny the wishes of a princess?" he teased as he climbed back onto the bed, crawling up my body and dropping kisses from the top of my foot, up my legs, and all the way up to my mouth. "You are the most beautiful creature I've ever seen. I don't know what I did in my previous life to deserve you now, but it must have been truly epic."

"You always know the right thing to say to flatter a girl," I said as I reached down and gripped his erection.

He sucked in a breath.

"But the time for pretty speeches is over. Now, now is the time to follow through on your promises."

Gently, he gripped my wrist to make me release him and took that wrist and put it above my head. He grabbed my other wrist, and put it over the first one, then gripped both in one hand. "I love it when you order me around, especially when it allows me to touch your body."

Stroking his free hand down my side, he brushed his fingers along my breasts and down to my legs. With a push, he moved my left leg, giving him room to kneel between my legs.

We both stopped when we realized he didn't have a condom.

"I'm not on birth control," I whispered, and bit my lower lip.

He reached over, grabbed his pants, and pulled one out. "When you admitted you wanted to mate with us, I thought it might be prudent to keep one on hand, just in case. Turns out that was correct."

Once he slipped the condom on, he positioned himself at my entrance and slowly, slid into me, stretching me to accommodate his girth.

"Yes!" I said and arched my lower body.

He groaned and dropped his forehead down to rest against mine. "You feel so good," he whispered. "So wet, so warm. So tight."

"No more talking," I ordered.

He pulled out and thrust back into me hard. "As you wish, Princess."

Continuing to keep my wrists captive above my head, he

kissed me while he moved. Sliding a hand beneath my lower back, he lifted it up, altering the angle, and the deeper access and thrusts had me throwing my head back, biting my lip to keep from crying out.

My orgasm exploded so forcefully that my entire body arched off of the bed with the intensity.

Trey grunted, pulled out of me, grabbed my legs, and pulled them off of the bed. "Onto your stomach."

Flipping over, I stood with my legs off the bed, and my upper body on the sheets.

He growled softly and stroked his hands along my butt and around my hips. "Perfection." Gripping my hips, he pushed back into me slowly, but once he was fully inside, he said, "Use the blankets to keep quiet."

I opened my mouth to respond with something snarky, but he slammed into me so hard and fast over and over again that all I could do was grip the sheets, bury my face into them, and try not to collapse as three orgasms back to back tore through me.

My legs shook with the effort to stay upright.

He slid his hand under my stomach and up between my breasts, lifting, he pulled me so I stood upright with my back to his chest as he continued to move in and out of me. Licking the side of my neck, he whispered, "I'm so close. I didn't ... I didn't think you would feel so damn good. I can't hold back."

"Never hold back with me," I ordered him. Taking the hand holding me upright, I moved it so he grasped one of my breasts. "Come for me, Trey."

He rubbed his face against my neck and shoulders, ensuring his scent covered me.

I moaned softly and leaned down so I was bent over.

He gripped my hips again and increased his speed, our skin slapping together so loud that I knew our attempts at keeping quiet were now ruined, but also not caring.

Another orgasm tore through me and I bit the blanket and screamed into it.

Trey grunted as he found his own release and stayed buried inside of me as he caught his breath.

After going to the bathroom to clean himself, he came back, still naked, pushed me into the bed, and curled around me, our naked, satisfied bodies, melding together perfectly.

"I love you, Lily."

"I love you, too, Trey."

"Tomorrow, I'm going to take you somewhere, okay?"

"Okay," I agreed.

"And tomorrow, Mason, Kayden, and I are going to show you exactly what we had planned when we finally convinced you to follow through with your promise."

"Tease," I whispered as my heavy eyelids became too heavy to keep open.

CHAPTER
FOURTEEN

The place Trey ended up wanting to take me was a jewelry store.

Somehow, we escaped the house without having to deal with my adoptive fathers, and after a delicious breakfast, they brought me to the very expensive store.

"What are we doing here, again?" I asked.

A beautiful woman in a pants suit walked out of the back, smiling wide. "Prince Trey! It's been so long." She attempted to pull Trey into a hug, but I hissed at her and she smiled and dropped her arms. "Are you here to pick up your item, finally? It's been waiting for, what, seven years?"

He had something here for that long? Seven years, that was when we were eighteen.

"I am," he said with a nod.

She clapped her hands together. "Wonderful! I'll go fetch it for you. One moment, please."

"Seven years?" I asked.

He nodded. "Yes, I bought this item seven years ago, but

it's been waiting for this moment." His phone rang, so he pulled it out of his pocket. "One second, it's my mother." Walking a bit away, he answered. "Hello?" His brows furrowed immediately. "You have no say, Mother. No. Absolutely not." His eyes widened. "You should not make threats you won't and *cannot* follow through on. If that's the way you feel, then perhaps it is better if I am banished then. Oh, now it's my fault? You know what, I'm done with your attempted manipulations and gaslighting. From this moment forward, you will not speak to me. Goodbye."

"What's going on?" I asked him nervously.

He dialed a number and held the phone back up to his ear. "Father, I think you need to speak to Mother. What did she do this time? Well, she just threatened to banish me from the Den and to disown me. Yes. Yes. Yep. Exactly. Well, from here on out, I'm cutting my ties with her. You'll have to provide her updates on my life as you see fit. She is not going to manipulate or change my mind, not again. I let her do that six years ago and I'm not going to risk another catastrophe happening." He glanced at me and said, "It almost cost me my soul."

Kayden wrapped his arms around me and pulled me back against his chest, his chin rested atop my head. "It's alright, Lily. He and his father are close, you know that. His dad won't let his mom's attempts at controlling him cause any issues with his place with the dragons."

"It's about me, isn't it?" I whispered, and swallowed hard.

He turned me around and brushed my hair out of my face, tucking it behind my ear. "You're the only reason Trey gets that worked up, so I'm assuming so."

Since Trey had marked me, and Kayden and Mason were part of his warrior's bond, I was now connected to the three of them. The connection hummed, fresh and powerful, providing a sense of safety and filling a place in my heart that I hadn't realized had felt empty since I'd taken the darkness back from them.

"Kay, are you upset?" I asked as I looked up at him.

He smiled, but there was a tension around his eyes. "Yes, but not at you. I'm upset about a lot of things that have happened the past week."

"I feel that," I said and sighed.

He kissed me chastely on the lips and said, "Feeling our connection makes all the pain and struggles worth it. I can't wait to be fully mated to you." Leaning down, he dropped his head down until his lips were beside my ear, and said, "Until I can cover you in my scent the way you're covered in Trey's."

I gripped the front of his shirt as desire rolled through me, making me clamp my knees together. "Yes, please," I breathed.

The woman returned with a black bag tied closed with a silver bow. When she saw that Trey was on the phone, she set it on the counter next to Kayden and I. "Here is the prince's item. Do you need anything else today?"

Kayden looked down at me and asked, "Is there anything you want from the store?"

My eyes widened. "No, I don't need anything."

He pinched the tip of my nose. "I didn't ask if you *needed* anything. I asked if you *wanted* anything."

"No, I'm fine. I have too much as it is and hardly wear it."

"Well, you're finally back in Jinla," the woman said, "so I'm certain you'll be attending more of the royal events soon."

So, she did know who I was.

"Thank you, but I don't want anything." My eyes started to drop to the display case where a necklace with a trio of diamonds that would hang down between my breasts was, but I looked to Trey instead. I walked to where he stood, scowling and whispering with Mason.

"Is everything okay?" I asked him softly.

Trey set his hands on my shoulders and smiled. "Yes, just dealing with my ridiculous mother. Don't worry, Father is handling it."

Turning to Mason, who had been silent the entire time, I asked, "Are you okay?"

Trey walked over to the counter to speak to Kayden and the sales clerk.

Mason looked at the ground a moment before he raised his head to meet my eyes. "The way the Grand Advisor acted, the way he so happily let us escape. It's been bothering me. I'm worried about our King and Queen. I know they're resistant to siren magic, but they aren't immune to it. The longer they are there, the more chances he has to put them under his control."

"I know," I whispered, and stepped forward so he would hug me. "I'm worried as well, but right now, there's nothing we can do, but wait."

In a soft mumble he said, "I'm also a bit irritated that I helped you escape, but you asked Trey to stay with you."

Wrapping my arms around him, I squeezed tight and said, "You know you earned extra brownie points for it."

He kissed the side of my head and hugged me back. "Mm, and how does one cash those in?"

"Ready to go?" Trey asked, interrupting before I could think of something funny to reply to Mason's question with.

Stepping back so I could look at them all, I nodded. "Yes." My eyes narrowed when I saw a new, second bag in Kayden's hand.

"Let's go to the house, I want to update some of our information there," Trey said and lead the way out of the store.

When we stepped out, a dozen reporters started shouting questions, videoing us, and snapping pictures.

Kayden stepped forward, using his body to block me from their sight and Mason moved next to him to add additional cover.

"What is the meaning of this?" Trey asked calmly.

"Is it true that Princess Liliana is mated to the demon king?" one reporter asked.

"Absolutely not," Trey snapped. "Where did you hear such an absurd rumor? Do you want to be sued for defamation with such a blatant lie?"

"There's a picture, of her hugging the demon king, them smiling at each other," one of them answered. It was a reporter I saw often for royal events and was normally very respectful. She pulled out her cell phone and showed us the picture.

It was one hundred percent a picture of Jol and I, just from yesterday. How did someone get a picture of that? There was no one there.

Mason turned and looked down at me. He whispered, "It wasn't me. I swear."

I nodded. "I know. The angle's not right." And I knew he wouldn't do that. My eyes widened, and I whispered, "The Grand Advisor, he must have other items, like the necklace, in Jol's room. That must be what the mana stones in the room are for." Fear coursed through me and my heart pounded so loud I couldn't hear Trey or the reports anymore. "He knows," I realized. "He knows the plan my parents and Jol are working on. He knows." Stepping forward, I grabbed Trey's wrist. "We need to go home. I need to get something from home."

Trey nodded. "Okay."

"Princess, have you chosen your mates? Are you and the demon hunters truly going to be mates?"

"Yes," Trey answered and smiled down at me. "Princess Liliana has officially accepted our request to be mates. Now, if you'll excuse us, we have pressing business to attend to." He put his arm around my shoulders, and led me away from the reporters and to the SUV we'd driven. "What's going on?" he asked.

"The Grand Advisor knows," I explained, my hands and body shaking. "That picture could have only been taken in Jol's room, and it was only Jol, Mason, and I there. Which means he likely has other devices like the necklace in the room. Which means he knows all about the plan my parents are trying to do. He knows, and that means everyone there is in terrible danger."

"Why are we going back to your house then?" Kayden asked as he started the SUV.

"I need to get the communication stone, to reach out to Jol, to check on him and my parents."

We sped through the city, back to the house. I ignored everyone who was in the house, running straight to my room and grabbed the stone.

Picturing Dad, I whispered, "Dad? Is everything okay?"

"Lily?" he asked.

"Dad, I think the Grand Advisor knows. You're not safe. You and Mom need—"

"It's too late," he whispered. "Jol has your mom and no matter how many times I fight him, I can't defeat him. Tell Nico I need him. I need him and Mom and Aunt Leona. I don't know how much longer I can last."

"Dad! Dad, I'm coming," I said.

Picturing Jol next, I asked, "Jol, can you hear me?"

"Little Queen," he growled. "How dare you contact me after abandoning me so long ago."

"I didn't abandon you. I visited you just yesterday. The Grand Advisor, I think he's been spying on you. He's changed your memory. Please remember. You have to break the magic that's in your mind, find the seam and tear it open so you get your real memories back. You have to see it, Jol. It's in your mind, changing the truth, trying to turn you against me."

"I trusted you even though the Grand Advisor warned me against it. I should have listened to him. Now, you've brought ruin to my world. I will kill you and everyone you love. I will take over your world, save my people, and destroy you and your family."

"Jol, this isn't you. You wouldn't hurt me. You have to listen. This is the Grand Advisor. I'll come to your castle. I'll come and—"

"If you set foot in my world. I will not show you mercy. In fact, you won't have to wait long. I'll be coming to your world with my army. Queen or not, I will cut your head from your shoulders."

Dropping the stone onto my bed, I gasped as tears streamed down my face.

This couldn't be happening. The Grand Advisor couldn't win like this.

Rushing downstairs, I ran into Branson, who grabbed my shoulders and righted me.

"What's going on?" he asked, scowling as he looked at my tear-streaked face.

"I need Grandpa Nico. The Grand Advisor, he's altered Jol's memories, and he has Mom and Dad. He said he's going to come and kill us all. We need Great Aunt Leona and Nana Jolie and ... and ..."

Branson pulled out his cell phone and started calling someone.

I dropped to my knees and Kayden sat beside me, pulling me into his arms and petting my hair. "It's going to be okay," he whispered. "We'll get this figured out. We'll rescue your parents."

"We have to kill the Grand Advisor," I said and wiped at my face. "But if he's as strong as it appears, he could pretend to be anyone."

"Leona will be able to help us prepare an attack against him. You know she is the strongest siren," Trey said, though he didn't sound as confident as I would have liked.

A niggling feeling in the back of my mind had me scowling. I was missing something. Something important.

Why would the Grand Advisor have brought me over to their world to begin with? Why this story about the necklace and me being prophesized to come? What role did I play in this? Was he just hoping to use me against my family? As a hostage? But then why let me live when he knew about my shadow powers?

There was a huge hole in this that we didn't understand, and it seemed like it was vital. So ... what was it?

An emergency meeting was called and all of the royals gathered together. While they talked strategy for an invasion, I stewed on what I was missing. Maya sat beside me, holding my hand. She'd rushed over after my brother had apparently called her.

Was there a memory from talking to the Grand Advisor that he'd made me forget? Did I have the information and needed to unlock it?

Closing my eyes, I searched through my mind and body, looking for any magic that was not my own.

There, in the recesses of my mind, a tiny sliver gleamed. It was so small I would have never seen it had I not been searching for it.

I tried to grasp it, but each time I did, I felt an extreme exhaustion cover me. Opening my eyes, I turned to Great Aunt Leona and said, "I need your help."

Everyone at the table stopped talking and stared at me in surprise at the interruption.

"What is it?" she asked and walked around the table to stand next to me.

"There's something in my mind, a sliver of something, but every time I try to grab it, I get tired and it slips away. I think … I think it might be memories from interacting with the Grand Advisor that will help us."

Mason and Kayden growled.

Her eyes widened, but she nodded, leaned her hip against the table next to me, and put her hands on my head. "I'm not sure I can do much. Although I've been practicing, removing a magic spell from another person's mind isn't something I've done. For you, I will try, but I don't want you to get your hopes up. You need to relax to let me in. It is going to feel weird to have me rooting around in there. Okay?"

I nodded.

She took a breath, and I felt her press against my mind and it took all of my willpower not to erect shields and walls to keep her out.

Mason set his hand on my leg and it helped calm my racing heart a bit.

She reached the glowing bit of magic and immediately withdrew from my mind with a gasp. Her hands dropped away from my head and she said, "Well, we've definitely confirmed that he's part siren." Shaking her hands out, she looked down at me and added, "I think I can remove it, but I'll need to sing, so we need to go somewhere private, where my song won't hurt anyone else."

"Go and help her, maybe her memories will help us in finalizing our plan," Great Uncle Silverowl said.

"We can go to the barn," I suggested. "If everyone else stays here, inside the house, the barn will be far enough away it should be safe."

"Sounds good," she said with a nod and headed out of the house.

Trey caught my hand, stopping me as I attempted to walk by him. "Are you sure about this? What if it hurts you?"

I smiled reassuringly, bent over, and kissed his cheek. "I'll be fine. Great Auntie won't hurt me."

"I'm more worried about what the memories will be," he whispered and stroked his thumb across the back of my hand.

"Whatever it is, I need to know." I kissed him on the lips and spun away, headed out to the barn.

CHAPTER
FIFTEEN

I sat on my rock with my legs folded as Great Aunt Leona put her hands on my head again.

"Try to stay relaxed, okay? Just keep reminding yourself that I would never intentionally harm you and we need to get this magic out of your head. Okay?"

"I understand."

After taking a deep breath, she entered my mind once again and as she neared the slippery magic, she started to sing.

Her voice was beautiful normally, but this song was haunting and had all my body hair standing on end.

Her tone changed, and a searing pain shot through my skull.

Clenching my hands in my lap, I grunted, but stayed still. Taking deep, slow breaths, I reminded myself this was my at request, and she was only doing what was necessary.

She began to sing louder as she tried to squash the magic,

but it wouldn't be squashed. Switching tactics and tones, she instead began to tear the magic apart.

Images, bits of memories, began to unfurl and my mouth dropped open.

With an exceptionally high note, one I was equally shocked and impressed by, she fully destroyed it and the memories flooded into me. There had been at least a handful of times that the Grand Advisor had visited me, asked me questions, and then tried to bury the memories. He'd also altered my perception of him, making me like him more and more.

One specific memory stuck out the most.

The Grand Advisor sat next to me, his hand on my head, and asked, "What magic powers do you have, Lily? What is your most dangerous magic?"

I shook my head. "I don't have dangerous magic. Just a dangerous temper. Or at least that's what Mom always says."

He sighed and rubbed his temples. "Even under my spell she's sarcastic and resistant. They really did train her well." Clearing his throat, he asked, "If I swore to leave your world alone, would you marry me and crown me as King of the Demons?"

"Eww, no!" I gasped. "You're so ... old. And evil. So evil."

"If I swore to leave your world alone and let the demons revive their world, would you agree to carry my child?"

"I just said I wouldn't marry you and now you're asking me to have sex with you? Are you senile!" I snapped.

"I never said you had to have sex with me. We can use artificial means."

"Why do you want to have a child with me?"

"I need royal blood. I need to break this damn curse!"

I flinched back, but he took a breath and said, "Don't worry, child, I'm not mad at you. I'm angry at the former Queen of the Demons, Third to Reign. She is the one who cursed me, who ruined my life! As her descendent, I think you're the key to breaking this, but I don't know how to break it, except make a deal with another, even more terrible being."

"What were those drinks you gave me? They tasted weird."

"Truth serums," he explained.

"Why would you give me truth serums?"

"I need to know about your adoptive family. Tell me their powers. Their strengths. Their weaknesses. Tell me everything about them."

Instead of answering him, I asked, "Why did my demon nana curse you? You probably did something bad."

He sighed and ran a hand down his face. "If no one you know can break this curse, then I need a royal child to raise and train."

"You can't use a child like that!" I gasped in horror and tried to move away from him, but my body wasn't reacting.

"I'll use whatever means I must, including taking over your world so I have even better access to magic users. Focus, Lily. I need you to tell me everything about your family."

"I can't betray them."

"Don't worry," he smiled evilly, "you won't remember a thing tomorrow."

"Fine, here's what you need to know. My family are going to beat you into a bloody, pile of pulp. They will do far worse things than whatever curse my demon nana placed on you. My

soon to be mates are going to rip your arms off and beat you with them for suggesting I carry your child."

"Shut up!" he snapped and put his fingers on my head.

I sat up with a gasp and locked eyes with Great Aunt Leona. "You did it! I remember!" She slumped forward, and I caught her. "Auntie?"

Smiling softly, she said, "I'm okay. Just a little exhausted. It's been a while since I had to use that much magic and those songs. You always like to test me, don't you little snake?"

Looping my arm around her waist, I helped her stand, and we headed towards the house.

Great Uncle Silverowl rushed out of the house and scooped her up in his arms. "Are you alright?"

She nodded and rested her head against his shoulder. "Just tired."

He looked down at me. "Did it work?"

I nodded and smiled. "She's truly amazing. Now, let's go back to everyone. I've got more details to share."

Once inside and facing everyone again, I shared my newly revealed memories. That started a huge discussion that went into the early hours of the morning.

I woke, my face pressed against a warm, naked, male chest. I bolted upright in surprise.

Mason blinked open his eyes, groaned, and pulled me back down to resume lying on him where we were on the couch. "Five more minutes," he mumbled sleepily against my hair.

"Breakfast is ready," Branson announced, startling me.

Trying to sit up, Mason growled and tightened his hold.

"I've got to pee, Mas," I grunted and squirmed out of his hold to rush upstairs.

After brushing my hair, teeth, and getting changed, I went downstairs to join everyone for breakfast.

"Was a plan of action decided on?" I asked Trey and took the empty seat next to him at the dining table.

My brother sat on my other side and shook his head. "They're still arguing about what to do."

Decisions did not come fast to the royals. It was one thing that used to irritate me, but now I understood. You couldn't always just rush in and save the day. Sometimes, you had to thoroughly plan out an attack as well as plans C through Z just to be sure you were prepared for anything.

"I'm worried about Mom," I said softly.

Tony scowled and stabbed his eggs a bit harder.

Trey set his hand on my shoulder.

Riddick had just walked in and nodded. "We know. Us too, but we have to decide before we act or we may end up causing more trouble or just putting everyone at risk instead of rescuing them. We would love nothing other than to rush in and get our mate, but what good would us rushing in and dying do?"

He was right, but it didn't stop my worry. I just had to hope that even as angry or upset Jol was from the lies, that he wouldn't kill my parents.

"We would like you to come with us today," Trey announced, distracting me from my thoughts. "Nico has promised to contact us as soon as a decision has been made and that they will not act without us."

I looked at Branson and Triston sitting down the table from me and they both nodded.

Triston drew an X over his heart, smiled, and said, "We promise not to act without you."

"And we promise not to lock you up again," Branson said with a wide smile.

I pointed my fork at him. "Still not over that."

Kayden walked into the house, a strange expression on his face. When he caught me staring, he smiled and asked, "Are you almost done eating?"

I shook my head, realizing that I had not even eaten a single bite yet.

"Hurry up and eat," he said. "We have plans we want to get to." He sat on the couch and pulled out his phone, typing fast on it.

Trey squeezed my shoulder, startling me, since I hadn't realized his hand was still there. "Eat, Lily."

Mason finished his food and took his plate to the kitchen. He'd been avoiding making eye contact with me since we woke up. Was he mad I got off the couch so quickly? Did I think I had been upset to find us sleeping together?

My thoughts distracted me as I ate, but I did finish eating, though I didn't really feel like I had tasted any of it.

The guys hurried me out to a waiting SUV, which Kayden drove. Trey had me sit in the front passenger seat, while he and Mason whispered in the back.

"So, what's the plan for today?" I asked Kayden.

He smiled, but didn't glance away from the road. "You'll find out."

My brows furrowed. "You know I hate surprises."

"And you should give us this without arguing or whining. We went through a lot while you were gone." He said it in a lighthearted tone, but the seriousness in his words had me closing my mouth and agreeing to give this to them.

I could deal with a little anxiety if it made them happy.

We pulled up to Trey's house and I stared at it silently for a minute. As I squinted, it reminded me of a smaller version of Jol's castle and a prickling sensation covered my body.

"Lily?" Kayden asked, breaking through my concentration.

"Coming!" I chirped as I threw open the door.

It wasn't until the door hit Mason in the side that I realized he had been walking by the car door at that moment.

"Sorry!" I shut the door and patted his arm. "Did I hurt you?"

He frowned at me. "I'm fine. You just bumped me in the arm with the door. I'm not fragile." His frown turned into a scowl. "Are you okay?"

"Right as raindrops on rooftops!" I said, repeating one of Mom's favorite lines. Thinking of her sent a pang of anxiety and fear through me, making my smile drop.

"She'll be fine. Your mom is one of the toughest people I know, which is saying something, since I know all the royals," Mason said and put his hand on my lower back.

I nodded and followed Kayden and Trey inside.

Although it felt like I'd been there recently, something felt different. I couldn't place it, though.

"Follow us, please," Trey said as he walked up the stairs.

I looked at Kayden questioningly, but he just waved me up the stairs with a smile.

With a soft exhale, I followed Trey, remembering they needed this from me right now and the sooner I followed, the sooner I could find out what their surprise was.

My heart beat faster as I followed Trey; curiosity thrummed through me like a second heartbeat. What were they going to surprise me with? Did it have to do with what they had picked up at the jewelry store?

Trey stopped in front of a door at the end of the hallway, spun around, and smiled down at me. "This has been a moment we've been waiting anxiously for. One we thought might not come to pass when you disappeared to the demon realm. I hope ... we hope ..." He paused, closed his eyes, drew in a deep breath, and said, "I'm messing this up."

This was the first time I had ever seen Trey at a loss for words or unable to clearly articulate his thoughts. He was nervous, but why?

Spinning on his heel, he pushed open the door and stepped back, bowing with a flourish. "After you, Princess."

The urge to look back at Mason and Kayden was strong, but I straightened my spine and walked into the room.

The room was relatively large, definitely a master bedroom, painted a dark grey with black trim, but was brightly lit thanks to a cathedral glass ceiling with dark wooden frames. There were also two glass doors that lead to a balcony where a cute patio table with four chairs, a swing, and a table lay. Lilies lined the walls of the balcony, giving it a garden feeling.

On one side of the bedroom was a door that I could see led to a bathroom, white tile gleamed inside. On the other side was a huge four-poster bed covered in a black fleece blanket with a white snake. A snake that looked almost identical to me.

There was another door, but it was closed and the guys stood in front of it.

"This room is gorgeous," I said as I looked up at a crystal chandelier that hung from the center beam, casting rainbows as the sunlight passed through it. There were a few pictures on the walls, and as I got closer, I gasped, realizing they were pictures of us ranging from childhood to this year. Some were images I hadn't even known were being taken recently.

"We are very glad to hear that you like it," Kayden said. "It took us a long time to figure out what to do in here. It took Trey even longer to order everything since he kept second guessing himself."

"We have another surprise inside," Mason said and pushed open the door they stood in front of.

Another surprise? The room! Wait, was this ... my room?

My eyes widened at the realization, and I wondered for a moment if I was in need of a true vacation since that had taken me far too long to put together.

They took my expression for interest in the room behind them. I was interested in that, but more shocked at this realization.

Trey walked inside, followed by Mason. Kayden waited a moment, blocking the door, and smiled sweetly down at me. "I've waited so long for this moment."

"You have?" I swallowed hard. Was it hot in here suddenly?

He walked in and as I followed, my mouth dropped at the rows and rows of clothing, shoes, jewelry, purses, and in the center, a table where a small black box and one thin, long wooden box waited. The guys stood on the opposite side of the table from me.

"Princess Liliana Rubyserpent, will you do us the honor of becoming our mate?" Trey asked, opened the small black box, and revealed a stunning ring with a giant ruby in the center.

I blinked. Blinked again. My brain finally caught up, and I quickly yelled, "Yes!"

All three exhaled loudly. Kayden leaned forward, hands on his legs. "What was with that pause, Lily?"

Stepping forward, I held out my hand, wiggling my fingers, and Trey slid the ring onto my finger.

He kissed my cheek softly, and said, "I love you, Lily. More than my dragon."

My breath caught. Saying he loved me more than his shifter form was a huge statement. It was something very rarely said and Trey was not someone to use words lightly, which meant ... he meant them.

Mason opened the wooden box, revealing six bloodstones. "We have been waiting far too long for this moment and don't want to waste any more time."

He didn't have to say they were also worried about the upcoming battle and the possibility of me getting sucked back to the demon world. It was said in the way his eyes were pinched at the corners.

"I agree, let's not waste more time." Stepping forward, I picked up the first bloodstone and turned to Trey. "I believe as alpha of this pack, you should receive the first one, right?"

His lip twitched as he nodded. "That is the protocol."

I nodded, turned, and walked to Mason. "Good thing I've always hated protocol."

Mason's eyes widened, he looked over my head at Trey, and then back down at me.

"You're all going to get one, so why does it matter who gets the first one? I love you all equally, so who cares who goes first or last? Just like I don't care which of you marks me first or last."

Mason's shocked face softened as I spoke and he smiled when I finished. "I'm just excited we're finally doing this."

"Me too," I agreed with a nod. "Now, squat down so I can put this bloodstone on you. Oh, where do you want it?"

"My face would be preferable," he teased.

"Not everyone puts them on their faces. I know some who have them behind their ears," I said as he bent over so I could reach his face.

"I want everyone in the world to know I'm yours and you're mine," he said.

Leaning forward, I kissed the tip of his nose and whispered, "Good answer."

CHAPTER
SIXTEEN

Once the bloodstones were placed, I could feel a stronger connection with them, their blood inside the stones, their magic, now embed into my skin.

We walked out of the closet to the bedroom and I barely got two steps before Trey wrapped an arm around my waist, pulled me to a stop, and nipped the side of my neck where his mark was. "While I don't mind who got the bloodstone first, I am going to be the first to mate you." He purred as he licked his mark and my body arched back against his body, craving more of his touch.

His hands slid down my sides until they rested on hips, he slipped his fingers beneath the hem, and pulled my shirt up over my head.

The next moment, he pulled my pants down and reached around to slip his fingers into my already dripping core.

"Already so wet," he growled and thrust his hips forward, pressing his erection into my lower back.

"Skin," I whined. "I want your skin touching mine."

"Orders, my goddess. What are you orders?" Trey asked as he rubbed his finger over my clit.

"Remove your clothes," I looked over my shoulder at Mason and Kayden who stood just behind us. "All of you."

"You heard our goddess," Trey said as he tore his shirt, literally, off.

Part of me wanted to correct him about calling me their goddess, but the louder part of me enjoyed hearing him call me that even if I would never be one.

I ached for his touch, felt cold from him stepping back to strip, but I bit my tongue as I walked backwards, towards the bed, and watched the three sexiest men in my life take off their clothes at my order.

The three of them were all naked and all fully erect, a sight that made my mouth water in anticipation.

But first, I wanted to follow my demon heritage.

"First, I have a dance to show you," I said.

They looked at each other, then back to me.

Turning away from them, I started my dance, it wasn't as graceful as I would have preferred since I was trying so hard to remember the moves, but it came back to me as I twirled around each of them, stroking my hands along their bare chests, and moving just as Talrinir had taught me.

The end of my dance had me standing before them. It was probably just my wish, but it looked like they were even more erect now.

"You are pure perfection," Mason whispered.

A connection seemed to have already formed between us, a slight, smoky string, that seemed like a demon mate connection.

"Trey, lay on the bed on your back," I ordered, feeling emboldened. "Mason, come eat me. Kayden, fetch us water and stroke yourself until I'm ready for you."

To my surprise, none of them argued, not even Kayden. They all followed my orders, quickly.

Once Trey was on the bed, I crawled up on my hands and knees, then took him into my mouth, relaxing my throat, to take as much of him as I could.

He groaned and gripped the sheets in his fists on each side of his hips.

Mason startled me when he slid his head between my knees and leaned up to begin licking me.

I moaned around Trey which made him moan as well.

As I sucked and licked Trey, Mason's licking caused the pressure in me to explode. I popped off of Trey, crying out as I orgasmed. Mason held my legs, forcing me to ride out the orgasm and causing my juices to drench his face and down his neck as well as my legs.

Satisfied I was finished, he slid off the bed, wiped his face with his hand, and then began stroking himself, spreading my wetness over his erection.

Trey moved behind me, and after putting a condom on, slid into me. I gasped as he stretched me in such a delicious way and arched my back. Trey gripped my hips and set a hard and steady pace, our skin slapping together loudly, and it wasn't long before I came, screaming his name. "Once more. Come again and as you do, I'll bond with you," he instructed me. He flipped me over onto my back, dipped his head down to kiss me, and pushed into me slowly. I tried to raise my hips to meet him, which made him chuckle as he stopped our kiss. "Greedy, goddess."

He began to move in and out of me, adding an arch to his movements to alter the angle. He stroked deep within me, building my orgasm, the feeling tightening within me more and more until it exploded out of me with a scream.

Trey bit my neck, marking me, and the bond snapped into place between us. For a moment, I felt his orgasm through our bond and it made my orgasm last even longer, my legs spasming and my heart felt like it might burst. He dropped his head to my shoulder, turning to lick the mark, and I shuddered with a happy smile beneath him. I realized that not only had that bond formed, but my darkness had merged back into his aura.

After pulling out, I turned to find Kayden with the waters and drained an entire glass in two gulps.

Once I set the glass down, Kayden pushed me onto my back and kissed me deeply, his tongue sliding along mine. I felt him push the head of his erection against my opening and arched up, spearing myself on him. For so many years, I had dreamed of this. Of being mated to Kayden and the others. Finally, that dream was coming true.

With each thrust of his hips, he thrust his tongue into my mouth, stroking it along mine. he sensation was so intense that I orgasmed within minutes. He pulled his head back, lowered it to my neck, and bit down just as he shuddered above me. Our bond formed and linked with Trey's and my darkness seeped into his aura as well.

"Sorry," he whispered as he pulled out of me and threw away his condom.

"Why are you apologizing?" I asked, scowling. What could he possibly be sorry for?

"For finishing so quickly. That was not the plan." His cheeks were tinged pink and I felt his embarrassment through our bond.

It was a bit strange to feel their emotions through the bond, but also amazing.

"You don't need to feel embarrassed. We've got the rest of our lives for long mating sessions." I tried to ensure my emotions were felt by him through the bond.

Mason handed me one of the water bottles. "Hydrate. I don't want you passing out while mating with you."

I smirked at him. "That's an awfully cocky thing to say."

He frowned.

"You think you can fuck me unconscious?"

His wide smile made my heart stutter and butterflies swirl in my stomach. He was a handsome man, but when he smiled like that, it made him absolutely breathtaking.

"I think that's a challenge for a different day," he said, unaware how much he affected me. "For now, I'd like to at least add my mark to your neck next to my brothers' and fully bond with you. Is that okay?"

I nodded. "Yes, please."

He laid down on the bed, his erection standing thick and waiting, and patted his upper thighs. "Hop on."

Climbing slowly up his body, I watched his hungry eyes taking my body in, dipping to my dangling breasts, and then rising to my face. "You are a goddess. Perfect in every way."

Placing my hands on his chest, I slowly lowered my hips

down, taking just his head into me, and paused. "How do you want me?"

His eyes sparkled and he said, "Ride me hard and fast, make yourself come until it's coating my lap and dripping down my legs."

"Yes, sir," I said and sat down as hard as I could, his thick shaft filling me and making me moan.

He cupped my breasts and rubbed his thumbs across my nipples. "So perfect."

I rode him as fast and hard as I could and he raised his hips to meet mine, adding more pleasure as we moved together. My fingers dug into his hard pecs, my eyes devouring every hard line of muscle before me. He had the most chiseled abs of the three of them and I stroked my fingers down them as I moved up and down, stroking my walls with his shaft.

"Like what you see?" he asked, one side of his lips titling up in a sexy smirk.

Nodding, I sat down harder, making him moan and making myself come. It splashed onto his stomach and he growled happily.

"More!" He grabbed my waist, flipped us over, and bit into my neck, on the opposite side of Trey and Kayden's marks, and thrust into me so hard I was certain I would be bruised, but not caring.

I threw my head back and screamed wordlessly as the third and final bond formed and we both orgasmed simultaneously.

Panting, we lay there to catch our breath. Once again, my darkness seeped into his aura, meaning all three were infected by me again. No, not infected, but marked by me. It was my darkness, my powers, binding them to me as Demon Princess. It felt ... right.

In my mind, I felt the three of them. I felt their joy and they felt mine.

Mated. Bonded. Finally. They were mine. I was theirs.

Forever.

CHAPTER
SEVENTEEN

I woke feeling sore all over my body in the most delicious way the next morning. Reaching up, I gently touched my three bloodstones in a triangle formation on my left cheek. Along my neck their three marks throbbed as well.

The happiness was sadly tinged with worry as a dream had startled me awake. A dream of me having to choose between my parents and my mates while facing off against the Grand Advisor and Jol.

Kayden blinked open his eyes, met my gaze, and yawned. "You're awake already?" My reply was cut off as he pulled me down onto his chest. "Five more minutes," he whispered.

"But I'm hungry," I whined. My stomach growled, confirming my whining was legitimate.

Mason rolled out of bed. "Our mate is hungry. You know what that means."

"It means we have ten minutes before she gets hangry," Kayden grumbled, kissed the top of my head, and slid off the bed. "Everyone, get dressed."

Trey climbed out and I watched the three gorgeous males walk, naked, out of my new room. It was quite an enjoyable view.

Rolling over in the bed, I drew in a deep breath, smiling wide as the scent of all three filled my nostrils. I could definitely get used to that.

Slowly, I got out of bed, too, and headed to my amazing bathroom to wash and get ready.

Kayden found me in the closet, debating what to wear. Without a word, he walked around the closet, picking out items, and set them on the table. "You should wear this."

"When did you guys buy all these clothes for me?" I asked as I started putting on the cute sundress, leather jacket, and sandal combo he had chosen.

"Honestly?" he asked.

I scowled. "Duh, of course I want your honest answer."

"We've been buying you clothes for years, but we were too chicken to send them to you since we knew you were mad at us," he admitted. "Pretty much everything in this closet was an item we purchased for your birthday, holiday, or just because we were thinking of you. We've been keeping it in here, hoping to one day bring you to see it all." He smiled wide, kissed my cheek over the bloodstones, and said, "I'm glad we were finally able to show you."

"I love it. All of it," I told him and hopped up to kiss his cheek. "Thank you."

He draped his arm around my shoulders and said, "Anything for my mate."

Mate. It was such a wonderful word to hear.

I thought they were going to cook me food, but instead,

we all got into one of the vehicles and drove to a restaurant famous for its brunch menu.

"Are you sure it's okay for us to be out? Don't newly mated groups usually need to hide away from people because of the possessiveness?" Mom and her mates had secluded themselves away even from my Nana.

"We are no more possessive now than we were before we mated," Trey explained. "We won't randomly attack someone any more than we would have previously."

That was not exactly comforting when Kayden and Mason were concerned. It did surprise me though that they felt so confident in their possessiveness of me.

My surprise grew when we walked to a table where Ezio, Grandpa Rhys, Grandpa Foxfire, Grandpa Deryn, and Grandpa Nico were already seated.

All five stood as we approached, wide smiles on their faces.

"Grandpas. Ezio. What are you doing here?" I asked as they took turns hugging me before we sat.

Trey sat me at the head of the table, opposite Ezio. It was a little odd to be at the head while the kings of our clans sat on the sides of me, but I had a feeling it was important in this moment.

"We wanted to celebrate your mating," Grandpa Foxfire said with his usual happy smile. "This has been a long time coming and we're so excited you four finally took the plunge."

"I like the triangle," Grandpa Nico said. "It's cute."

I focused on Ezio and narrowed my eyes. "There's another reason you're all here. I can smell it."

Ezio smiled. "You've always been a bright girl, which is what my slow-witted son needs." He winked.

"I'm not slow-witted," Kayden defended himself before realizing Ezio was teasing him.

"We've also joined you to discuss you having guards," Grandpa Rhys, ever the serious one, said. "You and Trey are royals and the demons have a keen interest in you. With this upcoming war, we're worried that they might try to kidnap one of you to use as a bargaining tool."

"A tool to be used to make Mom or Dad do something terrible," I said with a hard swallow. Almost immediately, Trey and Mason set their hands on me, comforting me with their touch. Kayden reached over Mason to rest his hand on my shoulder for a moment as well. It was still odd to feel their emotions through the bonds and know they could feel mine, but it was also really nice not to be alone in my feelings.

Grandpa Deryn's eyes widened. "A vision? You had a vision?"

Looking down at my hands in my lap, I nodded.

"Why didn't you tell us?" Mason asked.

"Is that why you were startled when we woke up?" Kayden asked.

"Tell us your vision," Grandpa Nico said softly.

"Was it Nana who had the vision that brought you to us?" I asked instead of answering.

"Yes, it was," Nana Jolie said as she entered and flicked Grandpa Nico's ear. "She would have told you if her mates hadn't come to meet you secretly, too." Leaning over, she hugged me and kissed my cheek. "Congratulations on your mating. We'll throw a party once we finish this demon business. Now, someone –"

Before she could finish her sentence, Grandpa Rhys stood and offered her his chair, then he went to grab another one from a nearby table.

She kissed his cheek as she sat in his vacated chair, folded her hands in her lap, and looked at me, her expression turning serious. "Last night, I had a vision. I saw Mason, Trey, and Kayden defeated by demons. A demon male gave you a choice, a choice between becoming his queen and ruling over the demons or losing your mates and our world."

My eyes widened. "That ... that is not the same vision I had."

Her eyes widened in response and her mouth dropped open.

A mixture of fear and worry filtered through my three mate bonds.

The waiter chose that moment to walk up and ask for our orders.

Trey and Grandpa Foxfire ordered for us while I stared at Nana, wondering how our visions could be different.

Once he was gone, she nodded at me.

"Hundreds of demons flooded through portals, focused on killing my mates. I faced off against Jol, their king, trying to convince him I wasn't his enemy, to fight the spell that he was under. The Grand Advisor defeated you and your mates and gave Mom and Dad the choice, give up our world or Jol would kill me and my mates."

"Has this ever happened before?" Kayden asked. "That two people have had two such different visions?"

We both shook our heads.

"Does that mean both might come to pass?" Grandpa Deryn asked.

"Or that both are versions you will each see from the Advisor's powers?" Grandpa Foxfire asked.

Nana Jolie and I stared at him. That was a very good possibility and one I hadn't thought of.

What if he was that powerful? Could he make my parents, Jol, and I do various things based on what version he was showing us?

"I don't know anyone that powerful," Nana said and shuddered. "I hope he's not that powerful."

"Have you looked into the curse more?" I asked.

She waved her hand. "Let's stop discussing this. We brought you here to celebrate and to convince you to let us assign some guards to you. We don't need to discuss other matters right now."

Our drinks came out, and I smiled at the mimosa with a strawberry on the rim. Nana had the same drink and we clinked our glasses together before taking a sip.

"So tasty," I purred.

Nana nodded and relaxed a bit against her seat.

"So, have you decided where you are going to live?" Ezio asked, a hopeful gleam in his eye.

Trey nodded. "My castle just outside the Den." He turned to me and smiled sweetly as he said, "We were able to finally show her the room we've been preparing for the last few years."

Nana smiled, her eyes crinkling at the corners. "I'm so

glad you were able to work out all of your issues and ended up together. I've been rooting for you four since you all met."

Mason set his hand on my leg and I felt his happiness through our bond.

I squeezed his hand and let my happiness show to them all as well.

"Neutral territory," Grandpa Rhys said with a nod. "That's a good spot since you're royals of different clans." He looked at me a moment before looking away.

Was he thinking about me being the Demon Princess?

"I'd prefer you were closer," Ezio mumbled, "but that is a good place."

"About guards," Grandpa Deryn said. "We have a list of suggestions and we would like you to choose three from the list."

"Three?" Kayden asked with a scowl. "You want us to have three guards? Do you have so little faith in our abilities? We've been fighting, honing our skills, for years."

"Even we had guards," Grandpa Nico reminded him.

I didn't join in on the conversation since it would make me feel better to have guards, not for myself, but for the guys. Yes, they were strong, powerful, and deadly, but more claws were always better.

Especially with the number of demons that the Grand Advisor could send over at any given moment.

We finished our meals, promised to send our chosen guard names within the next hour, and headed out of the restaurant while Nana and her mates teleported back home, taking Ezio with them.

"You've been awfully quiet," Mason commented as we walked toward our waiting SUV.

I looked up at him with wide eyes. "You're one to talk."

"I'm always quiet. You're not," he countered. His eyes darted to my neck where his mark was and I felt a surge of pride through our bond. Possessive brat.

"Out with it, Lily," Kayden demanded.

I opened my mouth to reply, but snapped it closed and spun around as my chest warmed. My hand reached for the spot where the necklace used to be, but it was gone.

Had that heat, the feeling of the demons, been me and not the necklace the whole time? Had it just unlocked my demon side?

"Demons," I whispered as a portal opened in the middle of the sidewalk.

Mason drew his sword and Trey and Kayden took warrior shifts, the three of them forming a triangle of protection around me.

Letting my scales flow over my body, I waited anxiously to see who was going to come out of the portal.

The black smoke continued to swirl silently.

"Is it one of the random portals?" Kayden asked.

"Opening right behind Lily? That seems unlikely," Trey said.

"I think ... it's an invitation," I whispered, and swallowed hard.

"You are not going through that portal. Everyone is still deciding how to proceed now that Jol is brainwashed and your parents are captured," Mason said sternly.

"Maybe I can talk to them, convince them—"

"No!" all three snapped simultaneously.

The portal closed and I felt a deep sense of despair fill me. Once again, I was unable to help those I loved. What good were the powers I did have if I could never use them to save others, if they weren't useful in saving others?

Kayden's arms wrapped around me, squishing me against his chest. "Lily, we are going to rescue your parents and we are going to save our world."

"We're going to save Jol and the demons as well," Mason added.

"I don't see how that's possible," I whispered, and rubbed my face against Kayden's shirt. "I hope it does come true, though."

"Come on, let's go to your house so we can help you pack," Kayden said and steered me back towards the vehicle.

CHAPTER
EIGHTEEN

The house was empty, which concerned me, but Kayden and Mason hurried me to my room to start packing.

"I am not prepared for this at all," I grumbled as I looked around my room.

Trey set a roll of bubble wrap and a stack of newspapers down on the bed. "Mason, come help me carry the boxes up."

Kayden grabbed one of the photos on my desk and wrapped it in a sheet of newspaper and then bubble wrap.

"Was this the plan for today?" I asked. "Pack up my stuff?"

"Yep," he replied and grabbed another picture frame. "The sooner we can fully claim you as ours, the better."

I rolled my eyes even though he wasn't looking at me and opened a drawer to start pulling out my clothes.

Trey and Mason brought several boxes and set them around the room.

Mason helped me fold and box my clothes while Trey

and Kayden wrapped my breakable items in bubble wrap before putting those into boxes.

Since I hadn't been home that long since returning from college, I didn't have that many things, but somehow still managed to fill eight boxes.

While they packed the SUV, I went to the barn and stared at my pond and rock. I knew I could use them anytime I visited, but it was such a sudden, huge change. Yes, I had known I would move in with my mates, whoever they were, when I did get mated. I just hadn't realized it would happen so soon. And while my parents weren't home. Or safe.

I needed to figure out how I could end the curse that was placed on the Grand Advisor without knowing what the curse was. It was obviously something bad, since he was willing to sacrifice a child to make a deal to end it. Or was that just a ruse? Just another lie added on top of the many others?

Kayden slid his arms around my waist and rested his chin atop my head. "Talk to me."

As we walked back to the house and into the living room, I said, "There is just too much that I don't know. What if everything the Grand Advisor said, even what I now remember, was a lie? What if Jol always views me as an enemy? What if the demons defeat us and take over this world? What if my parents are already dead?"

"We all would have felt it if our king or queen died," he replied calmly and stroked his hands soothingly up and down my arms. "Your dads would know if they died. The mate bond between them is strong, even worlds apart."

"I keep getting the feeling that there is something I'm

missing. Some major thing that I should remember or know that could save us all. Could end this war." It was like having a word on the tip of your tongue, but not being able to say it.

"Don't push yourself. Leona used her magic to help you, so if it had been there, it would have shown then. For now, let's go back to our house and get you moved in. The sooner you are fully ours, the better."

"Kayden, we're mated, I can't be more yours than I am now," I said with a chuckle.

"I want you moved in, your scent permeating that place, so that if anyone enters the house, they know you are ours. I want to know I will wake up each morning with you there. With you living with me." He cupped my cheeks and whispered, "We have been apart, separated, far too much in our short lifetime. I don't want a single day more to occur."

The front door opened and Tony walked in. When he saw us, he smiled and ran forward to wrap his arms around us both. "I'm so happy for you, Sis!"

Laughing, I patted his back. "Thanks, Bro."

"I knew you would end up mated to them at some point, but I didn't think it would take this long. I'm so happy it finally happened, though." He released us and smiled at Trey and Mason as they joined us. "Congratulations."

"Now it's your turn to find your mate," I teased. "I happen to know a female who is interested."

His brows furrowed. "A female interested in me that you know?"

I nodded. "You know her as well, but I think you are just blind to her affection because of how long you've known her."

His eyes widened. "You can't possibly mean —"

"A certain fiery girl we've grown up with," I said with a smile.

His mouth dropped open. "You're serious? Maya?"

"You should ask her on a date," I told him and my smile slipped a bit as I added, "while you have the chance."

He set his hand on my shoulder and said, "We'll get them back and keep the demons from taking over our world. Remember, you aren't alone, so there's no reason for you to stress about it or feel like you're responsible in some way."

"I am responsible, they're also my people," I reminded him.

"Just because you are part demon doesn't mean you are responsible for this," Kayden countered.

"Do you need help moving your stuff?" Tony asked, clearly changing the topic. Did it make him uncomfortable to know that I was part demon?

Probably better not to ask.

I shook my head. "Trey and Mason just carried the last items out."

He hugged me again and pushed me towards the door. "Go, enjoy mated life. I'll reach out if anything happens."

"Don't tell Maya I'm the one who let you know she's interested in you," I called over my shoulder. While I wanted to help my friend and brother, I did not want her getting angry at me.

"Take care of my sister or I'll tear your heads off!" he called back cheerfully and waved.

Mason and Trey waved at him from the vehicle.

"Ready?" Trey asked.

I nodded. As ready as I could be.

Mason opened the door for me and climbed in next to me. "We have one stop on the way," he whispered as he buckled his seatbelt.

"Oh?" I asked.

He scowled and said, "We've been summoned by King Deryn."

"Grandpa Deryn?" I asked with a frown. "Why did he summon us?"

"To formerly introduce us to our new guards," Trey answered as Kayden started driving.

"You guys picked the three without me?" I didn't really care who they picked, but I was very curious who they had agreed to.

"We didn't know you wanted to be part of the decision," Mason said.

I shook my hands back and forth at them in front of my chest. "No, it's fine. I trust your judgment."

"Next time, we will be sure to include you in the decision process," Trey said. "We're used to making decisions between the three of us, but we will work on including you moving forward."

"Thanks."

My phone beeped and when I pulled it out, I snickered.

MAYA: *Tony, your brother, just asked me out on a date.* o.o

Me: And you accepted, obviously, right?

Maya: I haven't replied yet. Is this for real? Did he lose a bet to you or something?

. . .

I rolled my eyes. This girl.

Me: *It's real.*

Maya: ...Are ... are you okay with me dating your brother?

Me: Duh, if you become mates then you'll be my sister!

Maya: It's a first date ... don't talk about mates yet

*Me: You should wear that black sparkly dress for your date & make him take you somewhere fancy. ^-^*

Maya: I'm going to reply and then curl into a ball and hyperventilate.

Me: bye!

"What are you snickering about?" Mason asked.

"Maya freaked out because Tony asked her out on a date," I explained.

"Little matchmaker," Kayden teased.

"What are your opinions on me working at one of my parents' stores?" I asked. "Tilly is going to be out for a while once she has her baby and they could use more help and it'll give me something to do."

"Whatever you want to do, we will support you," Kayden said. "If you want to work at a store, that's great, I know they'd appreciate the help. You don't have to work if you don't want to either."

Trey's phone rang, and he quickly answered it. "Yes? Where?" His eyes darted to me before he looked back down. "Okay. Yes. Understood. Yes, have them meet us there." He set his phone down and said, "Change of plans. Head to the baseball stadium."

"The stadium?" I asked. "Why there?"

"A demon portal was spotted as well as some demons," he answered. "Our guards are going to meet us there."

A demon portal?

"What type of demons?" I asked. "What did they look like?"

"I don't know," he admitted. "I didn't ask."

Scowling, I clenched my hands into fists in my lap, an uneasy feeling settling in my gut.

"How long will it take to get there?" Mason asked.

"Fifteen minutes," Kayden answered. "Trey, do you want to fly?"

He shook his head. "It'd take me about the same time."

Mason set his hand on my thigh and smiled at me. "We're together, it's okay."

Right, they could sense my feelings now, through our bonds. They were all strangely relaxed.

I nodded and leaned my head against his shoulder. "Right."

As we climbed out of the vehicle, two men and one woman walked towards us. They bowed and focused on me. "Princess," they all said as they straightened. All three were alphas, without a doubt, though I didn't recognize the two men.

The man on the left was short and solidly-built with tan skin. He had a darker, aggressive aura about him, wide dark blue eyes, a small nose, and a rounded jaw. His brown hair was pulled into a bun.

The woman standing in the middle was tall and lanky with fair skin, a crooked nose, and soft, hazel eyes. She was deceptively average looking, but I knew for a fact that she could hold her own in most fights. I'd seen her spar with Grandpa Deryn and land a few good hits on him.

The man on the right was average height, extremely muscular, had wavy blonde hair to his chin, and electric green eyes.

All wore jeans and a t-shirt and I could sense they were all hybrids, yet I'd never met them before, which seemed a little odd.

"Lily, this is Patrick, Piper, and Paul," Trey introduced, pointed from left to right.

My lip twitched. They'd chosen three guards with P names? Had that been a coincidence or on purpose?

"They are all elite soldiers that have spent most of their adulthood on missions for the kings," Kayden added.

"It's nice to meet you, Patrick and Paul," I said. Focusing on Piper, my lip twitched as I held back a smile and asked, "They let you out of the Den without a collar?"

She smiled wide and put her hands on her hips. "I got off for good behavior. Plus, they knew that you needed an extra strong hand, since you're notorious for getting into trouble."

"Says the girl who burned down the shed," I accused.

"You brought the matches!" she shot back, mouth open.

"You lit them!" I shouted.

We stared at each other a moment and then burst into laughter and met halfway for a tight hug.

"I've missed you. Where have you been, bitch?" she teased as she hugged me tight.

I patted her back. "Had to keep away from your stench or I never would have found mates."

We laughed as we stepped back to arm's length, hands on each other's upper arms.

"I really did miss you," she said with a pout.

"Well, now that you'll be one of our guards, you'll get all the time in the world to pester me."

"Challenge accepted," she said.

"I'd forgotten you two were friends before," Trey said and sighed loudly. "This may have been a miscalculation."

Piper pulled me against her in a tight hug and growled. "You're not going to find anyone better suited for keeping up with this one and who is willing to risk their life. She saved mine several times, so I'm in her debt."

It was technically true. I'd saved her from a snake when we were toddlers and saved her from Great Grandpa Dan's wrath on more than one occasion.

"I won't allow you to switch her for someone else," I said sternly, hugging her back and glaring at my mates while we embraced each other.

"They will all be our guards from here on out," Kayden added. "So, try to remember that you should listen to them since they'll be protecting you."

"I'll try," I said and smiled wide.

"What's the status?" Mason asked.

Piper released me so we could face the group again and focus on the task at hand.

"There are no civilians inside since there wasn't a game today. There were two demons we saw, the bull-headed ones," Patrick answered.

"Let's go, I'll talk to them," I said and headed towards the entrance.

"Do you think that's wise?" Piper asked.

"Talking to them?" I asked with a scowl over my shoulder.

She nodded and asked, "Can they even talk?"

Right, it wasn't public knowledge that I was part demon yet, not to mention all of the things we now knew.

"Can I trust them?" I asked Trey and Kayden.

They both nodded.

"We are your guards," Piper said. "You can trust us to keep everything we hear or see confidential."

I turned around to face them and said, "This may be hard to accept, I've barely accepted it, but ... I am part demon."

All three of their eyes widened.

"I'm the Demon Princess, actually. Apparently, my parents took me out of the demon world to raise me here. I am a hybrid of not just our races, but the demon race as well. So, please do not interfere when I try to talk to the demons."

They all nodded, dumbstruck. I don't think I'd ever seen Piper speechless before.

"Should we assign one of them specifically to her?" Kayden asked Trey. "Since she's the one who gets into trouble the most?"

I glared at him. "Rude, but we all know Piper is my assigned guard, so stop teasing her." Without waiting for them to discuss it more, I turned and finished the walk inside.

It was weird to come into the stadium when no one was there. It was so large and silent, super eerie compared to the warmth I felt when surrounded by cheering fans for games.

In the center of the field, a portal swirled silently. Standing just before it were two bull-headed demons, and just beyond them paced a familiar, floppy-eared female.

"Talrinir!" I called out and ran to her.

She grabbed my hands and inspected me. "You're okay?"

I scowled. "Yes, why would you think that I wasn't okay?"

Her eyes darted to the six men and one woman behind me and widened. She took a step back, but I gripped her hands. "It's okay. These are my guards and my mates. You don't have to fear them."

The bull-headed demons turned to face them and pulled out axes from their hips.

"Stand down," I ordered them and stepped before the bull-headed demons.

"Lily," Mason growled.

"We aren't your enemies," I told the bull-headed demons. "If you don't attack us, they won't attack you. Understood?"

They looked at each other, stepped back, and put their axes back in the loops on their belts.

"Talrinir, what are you doing here?" I asked, turning back to her now that I'd defused the males.

"Druth was taken by the Grand Advisor a week ago. He accused her of treason and we haven't seen her since. Then, this morning, the Grand Advisor and King Jolmach announced we would be invading this world in a week's time because you were taken hostage and we needed to rescue you."

"Rescue me?" I asked. "What sense does that make? Last time I spoke to Jol, the Grand Advisor had convinced him I was his enemy."

She shook her head. "I don't know what's happening, but the Grand Advisor's powers have ... changed. He isn't able to manipulate people's minds as easily and so he has to make the lies more believable. Everyone saw that King Jolmach and Zoman and Dhun care for you, so he couldn't convince us all that you were the enemy."

So, he made my family out to be the enemy instead.

"Have you heard news of my parents?"

"They've been imprisoned. Your father destroyed part of the city and your mother destroyed part of the castle while fighting King Jolmach. The Grand Advisor used a spell that stopped them and allowed their capture. I think they intend to use them as bargaining chips when they invade. To try to convince your people to hand you over."

"Hand me over?" I asked. Why? Why did the Grand Advisor suddenly want me back?

"Over my dead body," Mason growled.

"This doesn't make sense," I whispered. "What is his goal? What will he gain by me returning to your world?"

"Druth said it has something to do with a curse. One that the Third to Reign placed on the Grand Advisor," Talrinir explained. "It apparently causes him a lot of pain and makes it difficult to sleep. There was a rumor that he has been stealing magic from other beings to help ease his pain. She said you are the key to breaking the curse and once broken, we can break the Grand Advisor's hold on our people."

"How will breaking his curse free your people?" Trey asked. "That doesn't make sense."

Talrinir shrugged. "I don't know. That's all Druth told us."

"I don't know how to break the curse anyway," I reminded her. Pacing back and forth between the two groups, I tried to figure out what all this could mean. There were so many options and I didn't truly know the Grand Advisor that well. "Talrinir, was there anything else Druth said?"

She tugged at her ears a moment and whined as she thought. "Oh!" she gasped and spun to face me. "She did say something about blood and shadows being the key."

Blood and shadows?

I summoned the shadow snake and it blinked ruby eyes at me in its shadow body. "Do you know?" I asked it.

It bobbed its head.

My eyes widened. "You know how to break the curse?"

It bobbed its head again.

"How?"

The snake swirled until it became larger, then made an overexaggerated biting motion.

"You bite him?" I asked, confused.

"There must be a power the shadow can use once it bites and draws his blood," Talrinir said and smiled. "That makes a lot of sense!"

Something about her statement and phrasing bothered me. I looked at her out of my peripheral vision and my eyes widened.

That wasn't Talrinir.

How could I have been so stupid? Of course she wouldn't be able to come find me. Especially not with two bull-headed demons as guards! Idiot. I was an idiot!

Mason, Trey, and Kayden took a step closer, sensing my fear.

"Talrinir, I need you to do me a favor," I said quickly. I put one hand behind my back and waved at my mates to keep them away.

"Of course," fake Talrinir said. "Anything for you, Princess."

"I need you to tell the Grand Advisor that I will break his curse if he frees my parents, unharmed, and to this world. Okay?"

"I don't know if he'll listen to me," she whispered. "Especially since he won't want to give up your parents."

"Tell him to release my parents, unharmed, and I will willingly return to the demon world, break his curse, and gift him a mana stone with some of my magic stored within it. He can use that magic to do whatever he needs or wants."

Fake Talrinir's eyes widened. "A stone with your magic in it?"

I could practically see him salivating.

"You better hurry back before the portal closes!" I urged them, grabbed their shoulders, and spun them back towards it. "We know these are very random and the timelines for their staying open are even more random."

"How can I contact you again if I need to?"

I smiled and said, "I'll see you at the battle in one week, right?"

"Oh, yes, of course," fake Talrinir replied. "Hopefully, the Grand Advisor will accept your offer."

"Can you do me one more favor?" I asked. I had no idea if he would do this or not.

"Anything for you, Princess."

"Tell Jol, King Jolmach, that I intend to keep my promise."

"Promise?" fake Talrinir asked, ears flopping to the side as her head tilted.

I nodded. "He'll know what it means. Now, hurry, go!" I shoved their shoulders hard, making them stumble towards the portal.

"Stay safe, Princess!" they called back as they stepped through, the bull-headed demons on their heels.

The portal closed and I spun around to face the six scowling shifters behind me. "That wasn't Talrinir. That was the Grand Advisor."

"What?" Kayden snapped. "Why didn't you tell us? We could have grabbed him and ..."

"I realized it after I stupidly allowed him to find out I can break his curse. Plus, we don't know if we can withstand his magic. It's better if we play along with his ruse, so we can get my parents back."

"Do you think he's really going to trade your parents for breaking the curse?" Trey asked.

"I think he wants this curse gone more than anything else. Plus, once the curse is gone, he'll be able to use his powers fully again."

"Then we don't want to break the curse, right?" Piper asked.

"If I can get my parents back, I'll do anything, including breaking the curse on him, even if does make him more powerful."

"He's already extremely powerful," Mason reminded me. "Wouldn't it be better to try to defeat him first?"

"I have a plan," I said with a wicked smile. "It involves one of my powers I haven't told anyone about."

"How many of those do you have?" Kayden asked with a scowl.

"About six?" I said and shrugged. "They started showing up randomly while I was at college."

"Speaking of college, you said something happened while you were there, but haven't told us what it was."

"It's in the past, it doesn't matter," I grumbled.

"We need to know. We need to know everything about your past and your powers," Trey countered.

Taking a deep breath I admitted, "I almost killed someone."

CHAPTER
NINETEEN

"What happened?" Mason asked, worried.

"He attacked me and I couldn't control my anger," I admitted. "The only reason he's not dead is because Mom sent me a text and the sound of her message tone snapped me out of it. Not even my parents know."

"Was that when you disappeared for a week?" Kayden asked.

I scowled at him. "How'd you know about that?"

"Dad told me because your parents had freaked out. You told them you'd been in snake form and digesting, but I knew that had to be a lie, since it doesn't take you a week to digest anything. Not since you turned twelve."

He knew me so well; it was really endearing.

"Did you turn him in to get punished?" Trey asked.

I shook my head. "No, I convinced him to keep it a secret and told him if I ever saw him again that I'd give him to Caleb to deal with. Apparently, Caleb is scarier than me, even when I almost beat him to death."

"I would choose that over Caleb finding out I attacked his daughter for sure," Piper muttered.

I supposed most would choose me beating them to facing Dad's wrath. "After it happened, I noticed more powers that I hadn't had before, like the premonitions and the ability to tell when someone is lying."

"Wait, what? You can tell when someone is lying?" Trey asked.

I nodded.

"Well, that's incredibly handy," he whispered and got a far off look in his eyes, no doubt thinking of ways to utilize that skill.

"What else happened?" Mason asked.

"I was stalked by someone for a short while, but—"

"What?" Kayden asked and growled.

Mason smirked and asked, "Jealous it wasn't you?"

I dropped my head down so Kayden wouldn't see me laugh.

"Shut up, bird brain," Kayden snapped.

"So, now that this has been handled, shall we go home?" I asked and headed towards the door. "I have a lot of unpacking to do."

"Yes, let's go to the house," Trey agreed.

Once at the house, Trey and Kayden spoke with our new guards while Mason helped me unpack.

"You've been rather quiet," I whispered, and glanced at him. He was also stewing about something, switching between worry and anger, or at least that was how it felt through the bond.

"I don't like knowing that you were in trouble and we

weren't able to help you or be there for you," he answered. "If I had just gone to your college, spoken to you and cleared all of this up—"

"You can't blame yourself for something in the past and out of your control. There are a ton of things I would change if I could, but what matters is the here and now and our future."

He set down the picture in his hands and grabbed me in a tight hug, pressing his nose to my hair and inhaling deeply. "The only thing that matters to me is you, Lily. Keeping you safe. Keeping you happy. Being by your side. I should have told you I loved you before you left for college. I should have told you how I felt years ago. But ... I was too scared. I was a coward and I'm sorry. I was worried that ... if you didn't have the same feelings and now, I had made things weird, that you wouldn't want to see me anymore. I'm not going to let my fear stop me ever again. I'm not going to let you get taken away from me ever again. Losing you would be worse than losing my animal."

I hugged him back tightly, drawing in his scent, letting it ground me as I absorbed his words and the love behind them.

"No matter what happens, you'll stay by my side?" I asked.

He nodded against my head. "Yes."

"Even if I chose to live in the demon world?"

He pushed me back to arm's length and looked into my eyes. "Is that what you want?"

I shrugged. "I don't know what the future holds or what is going to happen."

Silently, he stared into my eyes for a breath longer before

he nodded. "If you stay in the demon world, then so do I. Simple as that. If you want to move across the continent, to another city, back in with your parents, or to the demon world. Wherever it is, I will go with you. My place is by your side."

Lifting up on my toes, I kissed him lightly on the lips. "Thank you."

We resumed unpacking and as I opened the box of my books, a memory occurred to me. I gasped. "The book!"

He frowned. "Book? Which book?"

I pulled out the journal I had been recording demon information in while in the demon world and flipped the pages until it was near the back. As I had recalled, there were notes written by one of the females, the one who had actually advised me to accept the shadow powers, the real Talrinir. There were notes about the Third to Reign's powers, powers that I now also possessed. It wasn't a comprehensive guide, since they didn't know everything about her powers, but it was enough to get me started and learn some things I did not know before.

"What is that?" Mason asked as he rested his chin on my shoulder to read the notes.

"Information to help me with my new powers," I explained. "I had forgotten about it until now. I think a left-over side effect from the Grand Advisor's brainwashing and memory sealing."

I sat on my bed, set the book in the middle of it, and summoned the smoke snake. It blinked ruby eyes at me and its tongue darted out.

"Ready to practice?" I asked it.

It dipped its head in agreement.

With a deep breath, I imagined the smoke snake growing, increasing from two feet in size to over six feet and becoming proportionally larger as it did.

"Whoa," Mason whispered.

The snake curled around my upper chest and shoulders, and I already felt an increase in power.

"Your eyes are glowing red," he whispered. "They're ... beautiful."

Rereading the information first, I then sent a thought to the snake, asking it ... no, *her*, to become my armor.

She swirled around me and suddenly, I had black smoke scales all over me.

I tapped my fingernail against one of them and was surprised to find it solid. "It's ... hard."

"That's what she said," Kayden blurted as he walked into my room. When he realized what we were talking about, he rushed over and tapped the scales covering my arm. "Whoa. That's surprising."

"Also, what she said," Mason whispered as he grabbed my arm and examined it closely.

I rolled my eyes at their silliness.

Kayden turned his hand into a wolf paw and tried to cut my arm with his claws, but they scraped against the scales ineffectively.

"What the fuck, Kayden?" Mason shouted and shoved him in the chest away from me.

"It's okay, Mas. He didn't hurt me."

"He could have," he growled and brushed off my arm like he could erase the memory.

"We need to know how strong they are," Kayden said.

"What else can you do?" Mason asked and turned to the next page in the journal, completely ignoring Kayden, a bit of rage still simmering through the bond from him.

I let the shadows dissolve back into my body so I could focus.

That page described sending the smoke snake to bite another being and inject a poison that could paralyze them for a brief period of time. Weaker beings could also be killed by it.

"Wow, these are some really beneficial powers," Mason said as he turned to the next page.

"Princess?" Piper called from the doorway.

"Come in, Piper," I called back, while reading the new page on temporarily disorienting someone by causing them to see and smell only the smoke.

She whistled and turned in a slow circle as she walked in. "This is a really nice room, girl."

"Thank you. The guys did a great job. Oh, where will you be staying?" I put my finger on the sentence I'd been reading, so I wouldn't lose my place.

She flopped backwards into a bean bag chair and said, "The three of us guards have rooms downstairs. So, you can just shout my name if you need something."

"That means we can have horror movie sleepovers again!" I smiled wide, remembering the fun nights we'd had together, Piper, Maya, and I. Speaking of Maya, I needed to find a night to hang out with her soon. I had been a neglectful friend with everything going on, but with the battle coming soon, I had to be sure she understood that she

was my best friend, to ensure she knew my feelings, in case ...
I died.

"Only if they can include alcohol now," she countered
with a matching smile.

Kayden's phone rang, so he walked out of the room to
answer it.

"What are your plans this week?" Piper asked. "Anything
chaotic?"

"I'm sure there are going to be a lot of meetings with the
royals to set up the plan for the fight coming in one week," I
answered.

Kayden came back into the room and nodded. "Just got
off the phone with Dad and there's a meeting scheduled
tomorrow evening. Also, they have asked that you go to the
mana stone store and take the day shifts for the next few days
due to understaffing issues."

"Understaffing issues?" I asked. That hadn't been an
issue before. Plus, was this really what I should focus on?
Running the store when the battle was so close?

"A lot of people are leaving the city due to fear about the
demons and the increased number of portals," Piper
explained.

I sighed and rubbed my temples while closing my eyes
and dropping my head down. There were so many things
going on simultaneously and not enough time or manpower
to handle them all.

How could I show that the demons weren't the bad guys
when they were literally about to attack us?

Everything was so screwed up and it could really all be
fixed if we killed the Grand Advisor. I wasn't sure my plan

was going to work, but I had to have hope. I had to find a way to save my people. All of my people.

"Read this next page," Mason said and slid the book back towards me.

The top had a note.

PRINCESS, *the necklace with the bright jewel is a royal heirloom that belonged to Third to Reign. It has many abilities, not all that I know. There was a rumor that the Grand Advisor took it and I am worried he may have manipulated it somehow. That necklace is important and can help augment your powers. I'm not sure how it works, but I know it does, and you should wear it during the battle. Also, the Third to Reign was able to give some of her shadow powers to her mates, which helped protect them.*

So, that must be what the darkness going into their aura was! And somehow, when I was younger, I'd done it as well. It made me happy to know that I hadn't infected them or caused them to fall for me.

I continued reading.

WHEN YOU ARE *in extreme danger, you can unlock a stage Third to Reign called Goddess Mode. Where she was almost all-powerful. It drains the user, though, so be careful when activating it. There was also a rumor that it was a one use only type of magic, though Third to Reign never confirmed that.*

. . .

GOOD TO KNOW. I turned the page and gasped at the title.

CURSES

Each curse can only be used once a day. These curses will remain in effect until the one who placed the curse, or someone from their bloodline, removes it.

Note: Third to Reign had many powers, a bit of an odd humor, and a large temper. Use all curses with caution and be very hesitant to remove curses still on beings. She removed those she felt were truly ready to have removed before her death. Curses do not transfer to kin of cursed. No known "bloodline" curses exist. I will write what she wrote about the powers as well as add my own notes.

Pain – Inflicting an individual with the pain curse will cause them intense pain periodically throughout the day and night.

Drain – This curse must be used with extreme prejudice as it will drain the cursed person of ten percent of their magic power each day, which can be multiplied up to five times, causing up to fifty percent magic drain. Can be used in combination with pain and called "Infection."

Stain – This curse will allow you to put a mark on an individual and track them, allowing you to look at a map and within a one-hundred-foot area, accurately point to their location.

Chain - *Not recommended! Caused plague!* This curse will cause the first person to become ill, weak, cough, runny *nose, throw up, and every person they touch will also be cursed with chain.*

Scatterbrain – This curse will cause the person to forget important items, thoughts, and plans periodically. Useful on enemy leaders to cause followers to distrust their leadership ability. Also fun to place on annoying siblings and mates for short periods of time.

Abstain – This curse causes little to no interest in food, alcohol, fun, and sex. Useful on annoying siblings, nosey mothers-in-law who keep asking about grandkids, and enemies. Hard to plan a war when you are sad.

Removal of curses – To remove a curse, ask the snake to "withdraw" the curse from the being. It will bite the cursed person and suck out the bit of power that is placed to cause the curse.

My eyes widened with each curse and note I read. She hadn't been kidding when she said Third to Reign, my grandma, had an odd humor and a temper. I could totally see someone using these for the wrong reasons.

So, the curse that was on the Grand Advisor. Was it just pain or had she combined it with drain for infection? If he was in pain and couldn't sleep, but was also weak and stealing other beings' powers, it seemed like he actually was cursed with infection. Could I use that against him? Could I just remove pain and not drain to keep him weakened? That seemed my best bet.

"Do you have an itinerary for her?" Piper asked as I re-read the curses and notes again.

"I'll print one out for you," Mason said and left the room.

"Can you print me one, too?" I called after him. How did I have enough things planned to need an itinerary? Had they been planning things without me knowing? I didn't know of anything I needed to do except the meeting and now the morning shifts at the store. It worried me that I wasn't able to go rescue Mom and Dad, but I knew going on my own would be handing myself over to the Grand Advisor ... and stupid. As much as I wished to stop acting as if everything was fine in our world, that was the only course I could take right now. At least until the portals showed.

Mason returned just as I finished my re-read and handed Piper and I a piece of paper. My eyes widened as I read it.

"Picture shoot? Why are we having a picture shoot?" I asked and looked at Kayden.

"To take pictures to announce our mating," he answered.

Oh, right. The public liked to see news articles and social media posts with pictures to announce royal activities. It was still weird to me how some people idolized us. Or perhaps that was just my imposter syndrome as an adopted royal.

Speaking of adoption ...

"I want to go to the orphanage this week, too," I told Mason. "Can I do that on ..." I read back through the itinerary. "... Wednesday after my morning shift?"

He nodded and started typing on his phone. "Of course. Are there any other things you want to do this week? I'll get them all added and the itinerary updated now."

"I want to have a meal with Tony and a night with Maya."

I also needed time to practice the curses and the other

powers I had. There were too many things to do in such a short amount of time.

"Okay, I'll get their availability and schedule something," Mason said.

Piper tilted her head to the side as she watched us. "I never pictured Mason for the secretarial type. I assumed that would be Kayden."

"Kayden hates creating documents like an itinerary," Mason explained.

"I make all the important calls because Mason hates talking to people on the phone and he has terrible customer service skills," Kayden said. "It's part of what makes us a good team. We make up for each other's failings."

"What does Trey bring to the table?" Piper asked.

"My good looks and charm," he said as he entered the room.

I rolled my eyes so only Piper could see, making her smile.

"He makes most of the business decisions, though we all discuss it," Kayden answered. "He's annoyingly good at convincing others to go along with the business decisions he wants and that's why we let him do most of the talking during meetings."

"He could talk a snake out of their scales," Mason grumbled. His eyes darted to me and he smirked. "No offense."

I smiled and said, "You say that like he hasn't talked me out of my clothes."

Piper threw her head back and laughed.

"Alright, it's time for food. I can hear your stomach growling from downstairs," Trey said and scooped me up off the bed and into a bridal carry. He kissed my cheek as he carried me out of the room and downstairs to the dining room.

I wrapped my arms around his neck and kissed his cheek just below his bloodstone. "You just missed me and didn't like me being up there away from you, didn't you?"

He looked at me from the corner of his eye before setting me down on a chair at the table and rubbing his cheek along mine, marking his scent on me. "Perhaps."

A huge amount of food had been prepared and set on the table. "Did you make all of this?" Had we been up in my room long enough for him to have time to cook all this?

"You lost track of time, obviously," he said with a smile. "Judging by your shocked face at the food on the table."

"And that you can feel my surprise through the mate bond," I added, since I could feel his amusement.

"I did have help," he said as he sat at the head of the table opposite me. "Paul is a great cook, probably should have been a chef of his own restaurant."

"Perhaps that's what I'll do when I retire," Paul said as he joined us at the table. "I can call the restaurant, The Alphahole."

"The Alphahole?" I asked with a soft laugh.

"That's what my girlfriends called me," he said and shrugged. "I have a feeling several other alphas I know were called the same thing."

"I bet that's not all they called you," Trey teased.

"True," Paul said, and the three of us laughed.

Everyone else joined us, taking seats around the table.

"Thank you for agreeing to be our guards," Trey said. "I

know it's not your normal type of assignment, but having you three here does make me feel a bit more at ease."

"Understandable that you need a few extra sets of hands when you chose the mate you did," Piper teased.

"We're happy to be of service to you, Prince Trey," Patrick said.

"Just Trey, Patrick. As our guards, you may address us informally," Trey countered.

"This week is going to be a bit crazy, and we really don't know what is going to happen after that," Kayden said. "The demons are nothing like we thought. We've been fighting them for decades and had a lot wrong about them."

"Like them being able to speak and understand us?" Paul asked.

I nodded. "Among so much more. They are trying to survive and coming here to get supplies, like food, because their land was destroyed and they aren't able to grow crops. It really is a wonder they've survived as long as they have. They aren't a race of evil beings like we always thought. They're just trying to survive. Trying to keep their race alive, yet being controlled by a hybrid siren mage who is brainwashing them."

"That's heartbreaking," Piper whispered.

"I'm going to stop it," I said with certainty. "I'm going to rid them of the Grand Advisor and help them rebuild."

"Just because you are part demon doesn't mean you are required to help them," Paul said.

"Since I came to live with Ember and her mates, I've been provided anything I want. I've had the best life an orphan could imagine. Yet, I have done very little with this opportunity. Knowing I am the Demon Princess, that my grandmother's people are in trouble, how can I not do *something*?"

"You've done a lot for orphans here," Patrick countered.

"I've created two orphanages and given them gifts periodically. That's not enough. Plus, that wasn't done with my money. That was still done through Ember and Caleb."

"You are not going to win this argument," Kayden said with a soft smile at me. "She refuses to accept her good deeds."

They started passing around the platters and bowls of food so we could fill up our plates while talking.

"What if the people here can't accept them?" Paul asked.

I scooped a big spoonful of green beans onto my plate before answering. "There have been very few people killed by the demons, whereas we have killed hundreds of them. I know it will take time, just as it took time for hybrids to be accepted. It is a fight that I think is worth fighting, though."

And definitely a hill worth dying on.

CHAPTER
TWENTY

The photo shoot took forever because Trey decided to be a prima donna and made us do four outfit changes, three different shooting locations, and the photographers took a total of one thousand and seven photos.

The poor couple was going to get a bonus with a heartfelt apology letter from me.

As soon as the article was posted and pictures shared to our social media accounts, we got a flood of excited comments and reactions. Of course, there were also the negative ones, but there were always trolls to be expected on any positive post.

When we arrived at Nana Jolie's for the meeting, I was surprised to find a printed and framed photo already hanging in the living room.

"Wow," I whispered as I looked at it.

Nana Jolie came up behind me and hugged me. "I couldn't wait to put this up. You look so beautiful, so regal and queen-like. And your men don't look half bad either."

"We love you, too," Kayden teased her.

"Nana, there's something I have to tell you," I whispered, feeling nervous.

"Everyone's finally here," Grandpa Foxfire said as he joined us. He looked at the picture and smiled at me. "We are very proud of you, kiddo. You got your degree, found mates you love, and you've been doing a lot to help figure out the demon war."

How would he feel once he knew my secret?

We joined the others in the dining room, one of the few places large enough for all of the royals, minus Mom and Dad.

Instead of waiting for them to start talking, I walked to the head of the table and said, "I have something important to discuss."

"We know you're mated already," Grandpa Deryn interrupted. "Congratulations, by the way."

"No, not that," I said and sighed. "But thank you."

"Go on, show them your power," Kayden ordered me.

"Another new power?" Great Aunt Leona asked.

"Well, the shadow one," I explained. "I've learned more about it."

I summoned the snake who swirled around my arms and flared her hood proudly. "Armor," I ordered her.

She flicked her tongue out and then covered my body in shadow scales.

Nana Jolie reached over and tapped her nail against the scales. Her eyes widened. "They're hard."

"Hard enough to withstand werewolf claws," Kayden announced.

Mason turned a glare on him, obviously not forgiving him yet for earlier, which made me smile.

"I can also curse people," I said after dismissing the powers, "but I don't want to get into that right now. I just ... I wanted to tell you who I am. Who I really am."

"This is definitely going to be a shock to our people," Grandpa Rhys commented. "We should keep this out of the news for now. Until the war is over."

"Speaking of the war, we have something to tell you," Trey said. He explained what had happened at the stadium and my plan to remove one of the curses so we could get my parents back.

They spent the next four hours arguing over how to organize the fighters and pulled out a map to sort it all out.

I helped Nana Jolie with gathering snacks and meals throughout since we all ate a lot and often.

By the time everything had been decided, I was exhausted.

"Take this," Nana ordered Mason and thrust a box into his hands.

"What is this, Nana?" I asked.

"Supplies for when you get home. Have a good night and don't stress too much about the battle, okay?" She kissed my cheek and shooed us out of the house.

It took another forty minutes to say goodbye to everyone, especially because my fathers wanted extra hugs, and get into the SUV to head home.

"Well, I think that went really well," Trey commented. "They actually came to decisions on things much faster than normal."

"That's because they've been planning it since the last attack," I said with a small smile.

"What?" Kayden asked as he started driving.

"It was obvious that they had all been discussing the plan already," I said. "Grandpa Deryn and Grandpa Nico rarely agree on things so quickly. Add in Great Grandpa Dan and tempers get heated every time. There were no tempers this time."

"She's right," Mason whispered. "They must have not wanted to stress Lily unnecessarily."

"Whatever the reason, I'm not mad," I said and relaxed into the seat. "It was a nice change of pace to have them agree on things."

"Maya is at the house," Trey announced. "I unlocked the door for her."

"Nice!" I shouted. I sent her a quick text to get the movie she wanted to watch first set up so we wouldn't waste time arguing over which one to watch.

As soon as I stepped through the door, Maya ran to me and hugged me, her bright red hair covering my face.

"I missed you!"

I hugged her back. "I missed you, too."

We walked to the kitchen and Mason set the box Nana Jolie had given me on the counter. "This is for you two for tonight," he said. "I snooped on the drive home."

Frowning in confusion, I opened the lid of the box and gasped. Inside were three bottles of prosecco, strawberries cut into star shapes, edible glitter to add color to our drinks, and a bunch of snacks.

"She really is the best nana ever," Maya said as she began pulling items out.

Mason put two of the prosecco bottles into the fridge while I opened the third one.

He kissed me on the cheek and said, "We'll be upstairs if you need anything."

"I'll be here, so don't wait up," Piper teased.

He glared at her before walking away.

Maya looked at Piper and asked, "Did you do something to get on Dan's bad side again? I know you're not crazy enough to volunteer to be Lily's bodyguard."

Piper laughed while I pinched Maya's side on my way to grab champagne glasses.

"Rude," I hissed at her.

"I actually did volunteer," Piper answered. "Who wouldn't want to be around this serpentine chaos goddess and the fun she brings?"

"At least someone appreciates my chaos." I put a strawberry star into each glass before filling it with prosecco.

"Help me carry the snacks to the coffee table," Maya ordered Piper.

"Only because you asked so nicely," Piper teased Maya.

"So, how was your date?" I asked Maya as we got settled on the couches.

She flushed, turning the same color as her hair. "Amazing. He took me to a fancy restaurant, to see a play I'd mentioned a few weeks ago, and finally to get ice cream. We talked about a lot of things and I genuinely had so much fun. It's just so ... simple to be with him. So natural, like breathing."

"So, Tony might be the one for you after all, huh?" Sipping on my prosecco, I felt a sense of relief knowing my best friend and brother would have each other if something did happen to me.

"I don't know about the *one*," she mumbled.

My eyes widened. "Who else has your eye?"

"Tony," she answered, turning an even darker shade of red. "The one from the club."

I nearly spit out my drink. "Really got a thing for the T's, huh?"

Piper and I laughed while Maya groaned.

"It definitely wasn't what I planned, okay? Tony from the club and I have been talking and dating, but I've always had a thing for Prince Tony."

Hearing her call him prince was weird to me since she never called him that while we grew up. He *was* Prince of the Hybrids, so it was correct and I supposed it was easier to differentiate which Tony she was talking about this way.

"There's also ..." She fidgeted with her shirt without finishing.

"Jaeden?" I guessed.

Her head snapped up and her mouth dropped. "How did you know?"

"I've always known you have a thing for him. It was so painfully obvious. How did you convince him to start dating?"

"I was helping him with his game and he asked me on a date," she admitted. "Apparently, he realized that I was helping him because I liked him and apologized for being blind to my affection earlier."

"Does Prince Tony know?" Piper asked.

Maya nodded and picked up a cheese cube from the plate of snacks. "I told him at the end of the date. At first, he scowled and seemed upset, but after a minute of silence he said he was fine with it, since it is so common for us. I mean, there are *far* more males than females in our world, so it makes sense."

And he was raised in a family where we had multiple fathers, so it wasn't something he didn't understand. He saw that Mom loved each of our fathers equally.

"Any others you have your eye on?" Piper asked.

She shook her head. "I think three is enough for me, thank you."

We all laughed.

I started the movie and we spent the rest of the evening enjoying each other's company. It was something I had sorely needed.

No serious discussions, no battle strategies, just time with friends relaxing.

I really hoped I had more of these nights in my future.

AFTER PIPER and Maya fell asleep, I went to the command center. Trey had recently installed a fingerprint scanner in addition to the key, so we could use either one. I was very happy about that, since I rarely remembered to take the key with me.

CATHERINE BANKS

I needed to practice with my new powers and with the battle coming up so soon, it was difficult to sleep.

As soon as I sat at the table, Mason walked in.

"Why are you still awake?" I asked as he sat beside me and wrapped his arms around me.

"The bed was empty without you," he muttered into my hair.

"Well, since you're here, are you up for being a guinea pig?"

He drew back and frowned at me. "What for?"

"I want to practice my curses and their removal." Before he could protest, I added, "I won't use the really bad ones on you."

"As long as you don't use the one that makes you throw up, go ahead," he said with a small, tired smile.

"If you're tired, we can do it tomorrow," I said quickly.

He grabbed my hands and said, "To be honest, I woke up because I felt your unease. If this will help you sleep better, than I'll do it as much as you need. Sacrificing a few hours of sleep is nothing if it helps you."

Moving from my chair to straddle his legs and sit in his lap, I kissed him deeply. "I love you, Mas. I know I don't say it enough."

He stroked the back of his knuckles down my cheek and said, "I see it in the way you look at me and feel it through our bond. Though, I do enjoy hearing you say it as well."

"I wish I could go back and change the years apart," I admitted. "To not be so childish in my reaction."

He shook his head. "If I were in your shoes, I likely would

have done the same. Plus, we're together now and that is all that matters. Now, curse me."

Laughing, I summoned my powers and ordered the snake to curse him with Scatterbrain. She turned into a mostly see-through shadow and swirled around Mason's head before returning to me.

He scowled. "I didn't feel the curse placed, but I can definitely feel a weight added to me. And ..." He frowned. "Wait, what were we talking about?"

"Well, that was obviously a success. Okay, now remove," I ordered.

She did the same motion, but this time I watched her withdraw a wisp of shadow from the back of his neck.

Interesting.

Mason shuddered. "Okay, that's creepy. I do *not* like how that feels."

"That was easier than I anticipated," I whispered in surprise. "I thought it would take me some practice to learn it, but it's ... natural."

"Probably because you are spiteful like your grandmother," he said.

My mouth dropped open. "I'm not spiteful!"

He smiled, draped an arm around my shoulders, and said, "Baby, you blocked me because Kayden said something that hurt your feelings. You're spiteful."

"Hmph." Since I couldn't argue against that, I just didn't say anything.

"Ready for bed now?" He stood and stretched his arms up over his head, exposing a strip of skin beneath his shirt and above his shorts.

"No, I think I'm ready for something else, though." I slid my hand up beneath his shirt and stroked his abs while looking up at him from my chair.

He lowered his arms slowly, eyes focused on me.

Stroking my way down from his abs to his waistband, I smiled as he grew hard from the simple touch. I gripped him through his shorts and he sucked in a breath.

"Good thing Maya and Piper can't come down here," I said and pulled down his shorts, freeing his erection, which was perfectly at the height for me to draw him into my mouth.

He groaned and slid his hand into my hair. "Fuck, your mouth feels good."

The bond between us caused me to feel not only my arousal, but his as well and instead of taking it slow like I wanted, it had me *needing* him immediately.

I gripped him at the base of his shaft and bobbed back and forth, relaxing my throat to swallow him all the way to my hand.

His grip on my hair tightened, but he held himself back from thrusting into my mouth. After another minute, he stepped back, pulled me up out of the chair, pushed my upper back so that I lay my chest onto the table, and pulled my pajama pants down.

I gasped as the cool air hit my drenched core.

"So wet for me," he crooned and slid the tip of his erection inside of me. "Fuck," he groaned as he slowly entered me, filling me up, and stretching me perfectly.

"Yes," I moaned.

Gripping my hips, he pulled back until he was almost out of me before slamming back fully into me.

"Yes," we both whispered.

With no more preamble, he began to thrust in and out of me, drawing orgasm after orgasm. My thighs dripped with my releases and I knew I'd need to change before I went back to the living room to sleep and I had zero regrets.

He flipped me over onto my back, raised my legs up to his shoulders, and thrust into me faster and harder.

I gripped his forearms and screamed his name as one of the strongest orgasms I'd had tore through me at the same time he came.

"Good thing this room is soundproofed or you would have woken up your friends," he teased.

"Good thing," I agreed, panting and smiling.

CHAPTER
TWENTY-ONE

"Princess!" two dozen little voices cried out when I entered the main hall of the orphanage.

It was lunchtime, so all of the kids and the adults who take care of them were seated at tables eating. I chose lunchtime because I knew I could find them all in one place.

The director, Ms. Brown, hurried over and gave me a tight hug. "Princess Liliana! We are so happy to see you again. Congratulations on your mating! We were all so thrilled to hear you have found your mates."

"Thank you, Ms. Brown." I smiled warmly at the sweet werewolf who ran the orphanage. She was highly recommended from Great Grandpa Dan, and when I witnessed her protecting the children from a hellhound, I knew he was right.

Turning to the children who were gathered in the aisleway, I said, "Hello, cubs. I've got a surprise for you all."

The children ranged from toddlers to teenagers, though

the two teenagers hung back, letting the young ones get closest to me.

"Presents?" Molly, an adorable six-year-old elf girl asked hopefully.

Mason and Piper walked in behind me carrying two totes each filled with presents.

"Presents!" I shouted. The children cheered. "Everyone be patient while we hand out the presents."

"Is he one of your mates?" Leslie, a twelve-year-old were-wolf girl asked me, her cheeks tinged pink as she looked at Mason.

Ah, the cute little thing had a crush on him.

"Yes, that's Mason. He's a hybrid shifter who can turn into a raven."

Her eyes widened. "Is that why his hair is that color? Because it's like his wings?"

Smart girl. "Exactly."

Antoine, a thirteen-year-old hybrid orphan, stood to the side, his focus on Piper. He had eyes only for Piper even as we handed out presents, which made me smile even wider.

I walked over to help pass out the presents since Mason and Piper didn't know the kids' names.

It had taken me an hour to wrap all the presents, and only ten minutes to pass them out and watch them open them, but the smiles, excited squeals, and hugs were all worth it.

Nessa, one of the two teenagers, a dragon shifter, sat by me and asked, "Did the demons hurt you when you were in their world?"

I looked at her in surprise. No one knew I went to the demon world except my family.

She flushed and whispered, "I had a dream about it. I have them sometimes."

"Have you told Director Brown that you have visions?" It was pretty rare for dragons to have premonitions.

She shook her head while looking at her lap.

"Why not?"

"What if it makes me even less adoptable?" she whispered.

The older you were, the harder it was to get adopted and once you became a teenager, it was very unlikely to get adopted instead of aging out.

I set my hand on her shoulder and said, "Having premonitions is a very unique power and one that is highly sought after. I think you should tell her, so that she can notify the dragons." I could see Grandpa Rhys wanting to have someone with her powers on their payroll for sure.

"What if I'm a hybrid?" she asked.

"Then my parents will be excited to know we have another powerful hybrid to join our clan. We can have you tested, if you want? I know there are a few hybrid families looking to adopt, and I know what a good student you are and can vouch for you."

The kids didn't know it, but I often reached out to families to try to find them homes and recommended specific children I knew would fit their dynamic. I also had extensive backgrounds run on families trying to adopt to ensure they didn't go to bad homes. One incident was enough to make sure I never made that mistake again. Luckily, the child had called me and with Dad at my side, we'd rescued her and the adoptive parents had been dealt with.

"What does the test involve?" she asked, her hands fisting in her lap.

"Oh, it doesn't hurt at all, Nessa. My dad is away ... on business right now, but when he comes back, I can ask him to come test you. It only involves him smelling you."

Her eyes widened. "King Caleb can smell if you're a hybrid?"

I nodded. "And he can tell you what mixture you are."

"Whoa, he's even more incredible than I realized," she breathed.

He was, and right now, he was in danger.

What was going to happen if the Grand Advisor realized I didn't remove both curses?

"What was your vision of?" I asked.

"You were in a strange castle with a hellhound and a man with horns." She paused before adding, "You hugged the horned man."

"Ah, that would be King Jolmach, King of the Demons. He and I became friends while I was there," I explained.

She tensed. "Friends? With a demon?"

"They aren't the bad guys we thought they were," I explained. "I'm not really supposed to say more, but I trust you'll keep my secret."

She mimed zipping her lips. "Always for you, Princess."

I one-arm hugged her. "Thanks, Nessa."

"Princess! I have a gift for you, too!" Molly shouted and waved me after her as she ran out of the hall.

"She's been drawing almost non-stop the past few weeks," Nessa said. "You're probably going to be stuck looking at a thousand drawings."

I stood and smoothed down my dress. "That's okay. If I came more frequently, she wouldn't have to go through so many, so I can only blame myself."

Nessa laughed and headed over to finish eating her lunch.

After waving to Mason so he knew I was leaving the room, I motioned for Piper to follow me.

"Where are we headed?" Piper asked, practically skipping at my side. It was clear she enjoyed being around children and was great with them, a side effect of being a werewolf who was part of a big pack.

"Molly wants to show me some of her drawings," I explained. "Her room is in an adjoining building, so I figured I should bring you with me."

"Look at you being smart," she teased.

We exited the building the hall was in and I had to shield my eyes against the bright sun for a moment. "Too bright," I whined.

Piper pushed me forward. "She's vibrating inside the doorway of the next building. I think she might explode if you keep her waiting any longer."

My eyes finally adjusted and I saw Molly dancing from foot to foot anxiously with a big smile on her face. "I think you might be right," I said with a soft laugh.

Once we were close enough, Molly spun around and raced inside and two doors down to her room.

We followed and my mouth dropped when I saw the walls covered in drawings. Molly had always enjoyed drawing and coloring, but this was an unusual amount for her.

Even more unusual were what the drawings depicted.

Stepping forward, I rested my fingers against a perfect drawing of Azgon.

"Do you like them?" Molly asked. "I keep getting these ideas and dreams and just have to draw them."

Piper turned with a drawing in her hand and showed me it. "Is that you?"

The drawing was of me in the demon world, standing inside the store talking to the store owner. That was when I'd asked him about the prophecy.

"Piper, go get Mason," I whispered urgently.

She spun and ran out of the room.

Molly's face fell. "You ... you don't like them?"

"Molly, these are amazing," I said honestly, and smiled wide despite the fear beginning to grow within me. "You are so talented to be able to draw so well."

Her smile and energy returned. "Thank you!"

I picked up one showing three large black portals in the park with me, my mates, and Tony facing the Grand Advisor and my parents, who were on their knees. The Grand Advisor didn't have horns and had slightly pointed ears though. His true appearance.

This hadn't happened yet. She was having visions, too!

What could cause two children in the same orphanage to suddenly start having visions?

"Can I take some of these?" I asked her softly as I stroked my finger across Mom and Dad kneeling.

She nodded. "That's what they're for! I drew them for you, silly! Oh, the most important one is this." Crawling on her belly, she slid beneath her bed and pulled out a folded piece of paper. Unfolding it several times, she showed me a piece of paper three times the size of the other, and this one depicted me, standing with my hand in Jol's, our other hands outstretched towards the Grand Advisor who was on his knees, head back with red light coming out of his mouth and eyes.

"Why is this the most important?" I asked her gently. She was only six-years-old, so I didn't want to frighten her.

"Because this was how you defeated the bad man. You and the horned king made him give back the power he stole."

"How did we do that?" I asked. I had absolutely no idea how to do that.

She shrugged. "You held hands and did it. Oh, but also this. It's a little scary." She handed me another piece of paper, this one she had hidden in her side table.

Jol stood over me while I lay on the ground bleeding, my hand outstretched for the portal nearest me.

"Can you tell me what happened here?" I asked her breathlessly.

"You and him were fighting. Then you got hurt by magic and crawled towards the portal. I ... I don't know what happened after that." She frowned.

Mason and Piper returned and he spun in a slow circle as he took everything in.

"Piper, please gather the drawings," I said softly. I folded the one in my hands, the one that showed me hurt at Jol's feet, into a tiny square and shoved it into my front pocket.

Molly folded the big picture and handed it to Mason. "You should hold onto this."

I hugged Molly and whispered, "Thank you for drawing

these for me. If you get the urge to draw more, can you have Nessa send me the pictures by cell phone?"

She nodded enthusiastically. "Okay!"

Once we had all of the drawings, we headed to Director Brown's office.

She sat behind her desk and frowned when she saw the stack of drawings. "She's never drawn pictures like that before."

"She's having visions," I explained. "Nessa is having them as well," I admitted to her as I sat across from her.

The office was small, a single desk with three chairs in front of it, a couch to the side, and a wall of cabinets for records on the children. We'd offered to build her a larger office, but she said she would rather the extra space go to the children. She had very few decorations, but there were several photos of children on their adoption days. Seeing so many of those photos made my heart soar.

Her eyes widened at my statements. "Visions? Both of them? What are the odds of that?"

"Very low," Mason said as he continued to flip through the drawings.

"I've asked Molly to have Nessa send me the pictures by phone if she draws anymore."

Director Brown nodded. "I'll make sure Nessa contacts you with any visions she has as well."

"I have to warn you, there is going to be a big battle in a few days, judging by the drawings, at the park. The orphanage is quite a distance from the park, but I would feel better if you took the children to the hybrid lands instead."

She took a deep breath and looked out the window at a

few of the children playing on the grass outside. "They don't do well with change."

"I know, but I don't know if I'll be able to stop the demons from invading. It's all very complicated and I can't get into it right now, but if you take them to my clan, I can promise to have guards there to protect them as they're going to be protecting those that aren't fighting as well."

She nodded. "Very well. When should we leave?"

"The battle is in three days," Mason answered. "I would take them the evening two days from now. I will ensure there is appropriate lodging available for all of them and you as well."

I stood as did she and we hugged.

"Keep yourself safe, Princess. These children look up to you and it would hurt them should anything happen to you."

"I will do my best," I promised.

As we drove away from the orphanage, I remembered the child in the demon world. No matter what, I would open an orphanage in the demon world. I would make sure that none of those children had to scavenge for food in the future.

I just had to take down the Grand Advisor and un-brain-wash Jol while keeping my family and friends safe.

Easy.

CHAPTER
TWENTY-TWO

Tony threw down his cards and growled. "You're cheating! Somehow!"

I drew the pile of money from the center towards me and said, "You are all just terrible players."

Bran Bran and Triston pushed out of their chairs, now broke.

"You have a tell, I just can't figure out what it is," Riddick said softly as he stared at me.

I smiled at my fathers and said, "Only one person has figured out my tell and since he's my mate, he won't tell you."

Trey laughed softly from where he sat on the couch reading some emails. "That was a threat if I've ever heard one to ensure I stay quiet."

In a sugary sweet voice I said, "I would never threaten you, my love."

Riddick put the cards away and asked, "Have you heard anything from Jol?"

I took a drink of my vodka soda before responding, "No."

I hadn't tried to contact him either, terrified of what I might find.

From the vision Nessa had and the drawings from Molly, it seemed like we were bound to fight no matter what I wanted.

I couldn't believe a week had passed so quickly and as the day grew closer, the harder it was for me to get good sleep at night.

"I looked back through those drawings, trying to find anything that might be helpful for the battle tomorrow, but nothing really stood out or seemed connected in any way," Riddick said.

"From them we know there will be three large portals and we've split our fighters up into six groups, one for each portal on each side," Bran Bran said.

Triston grabbed a beer from the fridge and sat down across the table from me again. "We've also confirmed, after much back and forth arguing with your great grandfathers and grandmothers, that you will be allowed to approach the portal with Mason in raven form on your shoulder, but other-wise alone. We will let you speak to the Grand Advisor, remove one of the curses, and not move until you give the signal."

"Once you give the signal, Nico will create a portal under your parents, and move them to the rear where Leona and the three of us will be, to verify it is actually your parents and not a ploy by the Grand Advisor," Riddick continued.

"I know the plan," I said a bit harshly. "I've been going over it constantly. Don't worry. I'll handle my part."

"If something feels off, get out of there immediately,"

Bran Bran said. "We don't want you endangering yourself any more than necessary."

I wasn't going to flee. No matter what, I was going to get my parents back and take down the Grand Advisor. They might be mad about it the next day, but I wasn't going to fail my people, either world of my people.

After a few hours of arguing, I had convinced my mates to lend me Mason's sword that stayed invisible on the wearer until it was drawn. I planned to keep it on my hip until I removed the curse from the Grand Advisor, then I would cut his head off.

Hopefully, once he was dead, everyone from the demon world would no longer be under his sway. Otherwise, I would have to try to convince them all that I had killed their beloved Grand Advisor for a good reason and not because I was an enemy.

"How are you three doing?" I asked my fathers. Without their mate and king, they were likely in pain and experiencing withdrawals.

"We're surviving," Bran Bran grumbled.

"Once we get them both back, everything will be fine," Riddick said with conviction. "It's the only thing we can really think about, other than trying to ensure you don't pull something crazy and put yourself at risk again."

"I didn't put myself at risk last time. The Grand Advisor teleported me against my will," I reminded him.

"I wasn't referring to that battle, but all the other times in your life that you've done something crazy," he countered.

Oh, right.

"She's going to have me at her back this time," Piper said. "I won't let anything happen to our beautiful princess."

"You better behave," Tony threatened. "You're the only sister I have, and I'll be damned if you die before me."

I patted his hand on the table and smiled. "I don't have any desire to die anytime soon. Plus, I'm very invested in finding out who you end up mated to. So, don't worry, baby brother."

His cheeks reddened and he pulled his hand back. "Just be sure to call for help if you need it."

We played a few more games, laughing and teasing each other, and it almost felt like old times. If only Ember and Caleb were with us to join in the laughter and fun instead of stuck in the demon world.

A tingling sensation spread from the center of my chest outwards, making me press a hand against my breastbone. What was that?

"Lily?" Mason asked as he and Kayden came over to me. Trey stood and faced me, a scowl on his face.

Everyone's phones started dinging with text message notifications at the same time.

Dread filled me as I pulled mine out with a shaking hand.

GRANDPA NICO: *The portals have appeared in the park.*

"A DAY EARLY?" Triston asked. "Why?"

"To try to catch us unprepared," Trey said calmly. "Everyone, get changed. It's time."

Rushing to my room, I changed into my fighting clothes and grabbed the few mana stones I'd prepared as well as secured the sword to my back. I also put on the necklace and felt a surge of power course through me. Hopefully, it would help like it was intended to.

We had to take two SUVs, but once we arrived at the park, I made sure to take my time hugging each of my fathers and my brother.

"Keep yourselves safe," I ordered them.

"Ditto," Bran Bran said to me and gave me another, tight squeeze.

Piper stretched her arms and legs and bounced on her toes to warm up.

Mason gave me a soul searing kiss before shifting into his raven form and landing on my shoulder.

The three portals before us were huge, which made me concerned that there would be more of the large werewolf demons or other large demons we hadn't encountered yet.

I waved to my family stationed around the portals, and turned when I felt Great Grandpa Dan approaching.

He pulled me into a tight hug, forcing Mason to fly around us for a bit. "Don't do anything rash, you hear me? You're my only great granddaughter and I don't want to face any more days without you. Let the older generations take the risks."

I pushed back and scowled at him. "You think I'm going to let you do something crazy just because you're old? Great Grandpa, I don't think so."

"How about everyone acts calmly and rationally and nobody tries to sacrifice themselves?" Grandpa Deryn said as he came over to hug me and patted his father on the back. "You ready, pup?"

I nodded. "I'm ready for my parents to come home."

He squeezed my shoulder and said, "We've got your back. Just call out anything you see or feel. We trust you."

"Don't forget to tell them not to hurt my hellhound, Dhun, and don't attack the demons first."

They both nodded and hugged me again before moving back to their places.

Mason landed on my shoulder and cawed, "Worried."

"Yes, they're worried about me," I agreed.

He rubbed his head against my cheek, keeping his beak away. "Love."

I stroked a hand down his feathered back and said, "I love you, too."

Facing the portals, I took a deep breath, and headed towards the center of the three, standing about one hundred feet in front of the first group of fighters. More and more arrived, taking their places and preparing for our defense.

"Center, bottom!" Nana Jolie shouted.

All eyes turned towards the center portal.

The Grand Advisor, wearing armor on his upper chest and legs, stepped out of the portal. He smiled happily when he saw me standing on the grass before him. No doubt, he saw me as vulnerable without any armor on my body and no weapon in my hand or visible at my side. I hoped he would continue to view me as vulnerable and weak as we approached the first steps of our defense plan. If he continued to underestimate me, I could use that to my benefit and hopefully, decapitate him.

Jol in full armor including helmet came out next, his spiked mace in hand. My parents bound in the chains that prevent you from moving were carried out by two bull-headed demons who quickly set them on their knees on either side of Jol, right behind the Grand Advisor.

Great Aunt Leona blew out a breath, sending calmness to us all.

Taking another deep breath, I centered myself, drew on the calmness of Trey and Great Aunt Leona, and did my best to keep my emotions off of my face.

It was time.

READ the third and final book, Their Princess (Her Royal Harem: Lily #3): catbanks.co/Lily

ABOUT THE AUTHOR

Catherine Banks is an award-winning, USA Today bestselling author who writes in several romance subgenres and has multiple pseudonyms. She began writing fiction at only four years old and finished her first full-length novel at the age of fifteen. She is married to her soulmate and best friend, Avery, who she has two amazing children with. After her full-time job, she reads books, plays video games, and watches anime shows and movies with her family to relax. Although she has lived in Northern California her entire life, she dreams of traveling around the world. Catherine is also C.E.O. of Turbo Kitten Industries™, a company with many hats including being a book publisher and store full of nerdy fun.

facebook.com/catherinebanksauthor
bookbub.com/authors/catherine-banks
amazon.com/author/catherinebanks

CONNECT WITH CATHERINE BANKS

I really appreciate you reading my book! Here are some ways to connect with me:
www.catherinebanks.com

Join my newsletter for deals and snippets:
http://catbanks.co/newsletter